Acknowledgments

To God, who gave me the strength to fight through the
tears and write this book with the hope
that no one feels alone in their grief

To my Mom, Trudy, and my Aunt, Jane, the
strongest women I know

To my Husband, Paul, who has stood by my side
through every laugh and heartache

And to Matt and Brandon, my guardian an-
gels who inspired this book

PREFACE

I remember everything about that day, what I wore, what I did, what I ate, and how I felt. It's so tightly entwined into my mind that I fear I'll never forget it. I wish I could say it was a happy occasion, like a first kiss or the birth of a baby, but it's not. It's heartbreaking. It's the death of Claire.

CHAPTER ONE

"Claire! Not only did you drink the last of the orange juice, but you are hogging the bathroom! Get out," I exclaimed.

"Laura, I'm sorry I finished the orange juice, but please hold on, I'm almost done."

I continued to impatiently wait as my perfect older sister Claire finished in the bathroom. Why did she need so much time in the bathroom? It definitely wasn't to fix her gorgeous blonde hair or to apply makeup to her flawless skin. I heard the doorknob rumble and out came Claire, beautiful as always.

"It's about time!" I yelled and slammed the bathroom door. I actually had no reason to be mad at Claire and yet, I was. Claire was the perfect older sister who has always watched out for me and vowed to keep me safe. Unlike some older sisters who think their younger sisters are a drag, Claire has always wanted to spend time with me by going to the mall, helping me pick out clothes, and giving me guy advice whenever I asked. I had no reason to be angry but then I looked in the mirror. My tight red curls constantly failed to be tamed, my skin was anything but flawless, and my figure, well, let's not talk about that. In everything I do, I have always felt like I was in my sister's shadow. I'm definitely not as smart, as talented, or as pretty. I've always assumed Claire was the favorite, especially by teachers and sometimes, although I hated to think about it, by our parents.

I tried to fix my hair as I examined the zit bigger than the size of Tennessee that now resided on my forehead. It couldn't be covered. I left the bathroom and collected my backpack. Claire was waiting in the living room for me, keys in hand, and ready to drive to school.

As I left the house, I noticed the fresh crisp air that greeted me. Fall has always been my favorite season, mostly because it meant apple picking, Friday night football games, and of course, the beautiful fall colors. I climbed in the car as Claire started the engine. I felt kind of silly, maybe even shameful for how I behaved this morning. Knowing Claire, she would ask if something was bothering me and how she could help. As if she read my mind, Claire immediately turned down the radio and said, "Laura, I don't know why you're upset with me, but let's talk about it."

I have always struggled with apologies because I hated to admit that I had done wrong or that in some way hurt someone else. I felt sorry for what I said, especially because it had nothing to do with Claire; in fact, it was completely based on events happening at school that could be explained in two words: Drew Harris. Instead of admitting wrong, I simply looked over to Claire and said, "You wouldn't understand." We rode the rest of the way to school in silence, a decision I would later regret for the rest of my life.

I stood by my locker looking at him: Drew Harris, tall, slender, dark brown hair, deep brown eyes, and a smile that made me melt inside. Drew has always been one of my close friends, definitely one of my closest guy friends, only second to Gavin Frost, my next door neighbor who I've known since birth. Unfortunately, it seems like Drew will never think of me as more than a friend. My pity party was suddenly interrupted by my best friends, Abby, Maddie, and Grace.

"Hey Laura," they all said in unison.

We were all looking forward to the evening. Our school, Richard's High Tigers were going to play football against our biggest rival, the Baymont Pirates. Abby, Maddie, Grace, Drew, Gavin, and I were going to hang out after school, go to the game together, and following the game, the girls were going to Abby's for a girl's night.

"I had my parents stock up on chips, dip, popcorn, and chocolate ice cream," Abby said enthusiastically.

"That'll be great! Thanks Abby," we all said.

The bell rang for the first period and I definitely didn't want to be late for English with Mrs. Olson, so I grabbed my books to go to class.

"I'll see you guys at lunch!"

The day was going rather smoothly, maybe even great. I was sitting in my favorite class, Biology. I have always been one of those science nerds and I knew I would always be. Today we were learning about the phases of cell division. I kept drawing out diagrams of the different phases and just imagined that at that moment, my cells were undergoing this intricate process.

"Laura, what's your answer?"

My teacher Mr. Thompson had called on me and I'm pretty sure that if I would have heard the question, I could have answered it. Nerd! Most people can't answer a question because they are daydreaming about cool things like the weekend, buying a car, or boys, but me, no, I was daydreaming about prophase. Before I could ask for Mr. Thompson to repeat the question, the bell rang. Yes, saved by the bell. I left class with Gavin, but before we went our separate ways to drop our books off at our lockers Gavin reminded me that he would "save a spot next to him for me." He's my best guy friend and Abby teases me all the time about how much Gavin likes me, but I don't see it. I dropped off my books and headed toward the lunch room.

When I got to the lunch room, I grabbed my tray and saw Gavin in the distance waving at me to grab my attention. I went and sat by him.

"What did you think of that bio lecture today? That stuff is hard. Well maybe not for you Laura, you're a scientific genius," Gavin commented.

In hopes of looking somewhat less nerdy, I responded by saying, "Genius? I wasn't able to answer the last question." Unfortunately, Gavin saw right through me and explained that I obviously knew but had been daydreaming about science. Wow, he knows me too well.

"So Laura, want to hang out this weekend? I was thinking maybe a movie at my place," he said.

I smiled, "Can I pick it?"

"Please, no chick flicks, you can watch those with Abby, Grace, and Maddie."

"Ok, no chick flicks, but please, no macho guy movies."

"Ok, we can compromise on some comedy."

"Sounds good to me."

Just then Abby, Grace, Maddie, and Drew approached to sit with us. We continued to all talk and discuss our after school plans of getting ice cream and going to the football game together. I saw Claire had just walked into the lunch room and for some reason, I really felt like I should go apologize to her. I looked at my watch. Only two minutes before the bell would ring, but I guessed a quick apology was better than no apology. I excused myself from the group and went over to Claire.

"Claire, can we talk about this morning?"

"Laura, don't worry about it. How about we talk tomorrow after your sleep-over? The bell is going to ring soon anyways."

"Ok, tomorrow."

Seconds later the bell rang and still, no apology.

After school, Gavin, Drew, Abby, Grace, Maddie, and I walked to Tony's Pizzeria to hang out before heading to the big football game. We ordered our large pepperoni pizza and sat down.

"So, what is everyone's weekend plans?" I asked. "Hopefully it doesn't include a lot of homework."

Abby started out by mentioning the sleepover but then said her weekend would be pretty boring. Grace mentioned that she was going over to her grandma's house on Sunday. Drew planned on playing basketball with his brothers. Maddie boringly offered up that she had no plans. Gavin explained that he had no plans, well, except to hang out with me on Saturday. With that, Abby shot me a look almost immediately. Finally, I explained that in addition to the sleepover and seeing Gavin that I would be sitting around with family on Sunday. Finally, the pizza arrived and we all dug in.

That night after the game was finished, Grace, Maddie, Abby, and I went to find Abby's parents to get a ride. As we were walking down the bleachers, I saw Claire hugging her boyfriend, Kyle, who was the star quarterback. I walked over to congratulate Kyle on making the winning touchdown.

"Hey, great job Kyle. You're the hero of the game."

"No, we all did a great job," he said. "I just happened to make the final touchdown."

Kyle was a humble and genuinely nice guy. He was perfect for Claire, and everyone knew it. Claire and Kyle have been together for three years now and we all imagined that one day they would get married; in fact, I'm pretty sure they had already discussed and planned this.

I asked what they were doing tonight and Claire explained they were going to get some food and then hang out at Kyle's house to watch a movie. Abby was nudging me to say that her parents were waiting and I told her I would catch up.

"Um, Claire, about this morning."

Before I could finish, Claire said, "Laura, it's no big deal, go catch up with your friends. We can talk tomorrow." She smiled at me, and then I said goodbye.

We enthusiastically stormed into Abby's house still chanting "Tigers, Tigers, Tigers!" After the excitement of winning wore off, we began to settle down for a relaxing girls night. We started out by raiding the fridge for beverages and finding everything in the cupboard that contained chocolate. We began the night with truth or dare, and of course, like clockwork, Maddie asked me a truth about who I like.

"You guys know I am head over heels for Drew!"

Maddie laughed, "Laura, are you blind? Gavin totally likes you and you are just ignoring him!"

"What are you talking about, Gavin? We are just friends."

"Friends now, but Gavin wants to be more. Can't you tell," asked Grace.

"But I like Drew."

"Sure Drew is nice, but don't you see that Gavin and you would be perfect," Abby interjected, "You have the same interests and you both love spending time together."

"No, we don't."

"Aren't you spending time together tomorrow night," Grace blurted.

"As friends."

"Did you hang out at all this week," Maddie questioned.

"Well yes."

"Admit it, you like being with Gavin," Grace insisted. "You just haven't thought about him in that way because you've been all about Drew since the seventh grade."

I guess they were all right. I've liked Drew for two years now and haven't really paid any attention to anyone else. I've never thought of Gavin like that though and I questioned whether I could.

Changing the topic, I said, "Ok, enough about me, let's put someone else in the hot seat."

We continued to play truth and dare until we became too sleepy and decided to watch a movie, "Luckiest Love," the brand new romantic comedy starring Scottie West. As we popped in the movie, the doorbell rang. I looked at the clock, midnight. Hm... kind of late for visitors, I thought. Abby was about to run upstairs to check until she heard her parents rousing out of bed to go to the door. After a minute, I heard someone coming down the stairs. I looked and my initial thought was how similar the figures looked to my parents. I took a double take. Wait, it was my parents. My stomach immediately dropped. I knew something was wrong. Maybe Tofty, our golden retriever was sick. What if Tofty had died? We've had him since I was five, and he was part of the family. I don't know how I'd deal with him being gone. My mind was racing a million miles per minute. I carefully stood and looked at my mom. Her face was red from tears and her body was shaking in pain. Then I glanced at my dad and noticed that even he, the man who never cries, was shedding tears. At that moment I knew it wasn't Tofty, but all I could do was to stand speechless, afraid to talk and even more afraid to hear what they had to say.

Finally, my dad broke the silence, "Laura honey, there was an accident. Claire and Kyle. Kyle is in the hospital but....Claire, she, was really hurt. Laura, she didn't make it."

The words stabbed me like sharded glass pointed straight at my heart. Everything around me seemed to fade into nothingness. All I could say was, "Claire." My mom stepped forward to hug me but before I could feel her embrace, I was on the floor repeating "no" over and over and over again. My 18-year-old sister could not be... no, I won't even say it. It was not possible.

When I started to maintain composure, I asked how it happened. I felt so confused because Kyle was such a careful driver, especially when Claire was in the car. My dad cleared his throat and explained that it was a two-car accident and the police believe that the man in the other car had been drinking. Kyle must have seen the swerving man coming towards him and turned his car in hopes of avoiding him, but the man collided into the passenger side, right where Claire had been sitting. He said that she died instantly. She didn't know she was dying. There was no pain. She was with God now.

All of his words seemed fragmented in my mind... no pain,

dead, with God. It all pointed to one conclusion: Claire was gone, forever. I wouldn't be seeing her again. I wouldn't be seeing her beautiful smile or hearing her laugh. I wouldn't be hearing her soft and gentle voice. I wouldn't be watching movies with her, shopping with her, or simply talking about sister stuff with her. I was 15 year old Laura Russell, high school freshman, flute player, science lover, and now the only person my age that I knew of who was going to have to bury a sibling.

My parents helped me stand and said it was time to go home. All I could mumble was that I needed to collect my stuff and that the party wasn't over. Abby's parents, Mr. and Mrs. Bryant, said that they would bring my stuff tomorrow morning. I looked at Abby, Grace, and Maddie. They stood motionless as if wondering what to do. Finally, Abby came forward to hug me and assured me that she would stop to see me tomorrow. Grace and Maddie quickly followed suit. I started walking up the stairs with my parents. As we walked to the car, my mom grabbed my hand to hold, something we haven't done since I was five. I didn't know what to say and neither did they. All I knew was that my life was suddenly different. I couldn't imagine that this morning my biggest worry was the zit on my forehead and how to get Drew Harris to look at me as more than a friend. Little did I know when I woke up this morning that today, October second, would be the worst day of my life.

We drove back to the house in silence, and when we arrived, we gathered in the living room and sat there in silence all night long without sleeping.

CHAPTER TWO

The sun started to peer in the windows and yet, my parents and I were still sitting still in the same places we had found ourselves just six hours earlier. Around eight in the morning, the phone rang and it seemed to ring non-stop for an hour. Family members, friends, neighbors, and members of our church started to arrive at nine.

I decided to take a break and go take a shower. As I climbed the stairs, I was instantly hit with the reality that I would be entering the bathroom that Claire and I had shared. That was our bathroom. When I reached the top of the stairs, I looked down the hall at Claire's bedroom door and thought I heard a noise coming from her room. I cringed at the thought only to realize that maybe it was all a nightmare. Quickly running down the hall, I threw the door open and looked around half expecting to see Claire sitting up in her bed, possibly reading a book or maybe writing in her journal. There was no Claire. There had been no noise. One thing definitely struck me immediately: Claire's bed was not made. She always made her bed, so why wouldn't she have made it yesterday morning? The thought made me sick to my stomach. What if it was because she was preoccupied with how I had treated her? Maybe she was too worried about what was bothering me? I looked at my watch. About twenty-five hours ago I was riding with Claire to school. About twenty-six hours ago I had acted like a fool and treated her awfully. About twenty-two hours ago I had decided to apologize, but I never had the chance. I wanted to take it all back. I wanted to take her back. I wanted my sister here, with me, now, forever, until we were old, wrinkly, and in the nursing home together. The silence of the room scared me so I quickly ran back to mine. I continued with my plans to take a shower, but my shower became more of a crying retreat from everyone downstairs rather than an actual shower. I don't even remember if I washed my hair.

When I climbed out of the shower, I got dressed and examined my eyes in the mirror. Red, definitely red. And inflamed! I could barely see through my little squinty eyes. Would everyone know that I had been crying? Would anyone say something if they could tell? I decided to stay in my room until the redness dissipated. When I finally went downstairs, I was surprised that the number of people who had arrived had dramatically gone up. Feeling that all eyes were on me, I went outside to grab the paper. When I picked up the paper, I immediately saw Claire's bright blue eyes staring back at me. I caught my breath as I looked at Claire, realizing that I couldn't escape my new reality. The front page was about the accident. I walked towards the house and sat on our steps to read the article.

"Claire Russell, a seventeen-year-old senior at Richard's High, was killed suddenly in a car accident last night, October second at eleven p.m. Although Jefferson County police have not released a full accident report, they have revealed that it was a two-car accident. The first car, a 2000 Chevy Malibu, driven by Kyle Williams, 18, with passenger Claire Russell was traveling southbound on Hwy 35 when a 2003 Ford Escape driven by Alex Smith, 55, crossed the center-line and hit Williams car on the passenger side. Russell was killed instantly. Williams and Smith were transported to Jefferson County Hospital where they both remain in critical condition. Police believe that alcohol may have been a factor in the accident. More details will be published as they become available."

Below the article were three pictures. The first was one of Claire's senior pictures. Her blonde hair was down, her blue eyes glistened, and she looked so casual and natural in her blue jeans and nice green shirt. She looked so youthful, so full of life, and yet, life was the one thing she now lacked. Next to the picture of Claire was a picture of Kyle. He was in his football jersey and despite the masculine and intimidating persona most football players try to have, Kyle was sporting a huge smile. The final picture was of the accident scene. Kyle's car was completely totaled. The damage in the passenger side of his car was heart-breaking. From the amount of damage, it seemed that there was no way that Claire could have suffered because she had to have died instantly. That thought brought me a strange comfort during this terrible time.

I went into the house and set the paper on the counter. I knew that my parents didn't need a reminder that their daughter was gone, so I decided there was no need to immediately show them. I was headed back upstairs when my dad stopped me.

"Laura, your mom and I need to go to the funeral home. Do you want to go with?" He asked.

It had all happened so suddenly that I failed to realize that Claire's body didn't just disappear. She was somewhere, and we wouldn't just move on, but there would be a funeral. The question resounded in my mind, "Want to go with?" All I could think was, not really! Why would I have any desire to see Claire? All I could respond was "Yes." As much as I didn't want to face reality, I knew that my parents needed me there. My Aunt Christine and Uncle William drove my parents and me to Taylor Funeral home. My grandma had died five years ago so I had been to a funeral home, but I was only ten and didn't remember much. Furthermore, my grandma had been really sick with cancer and we had all known she was going to die. This was different.

We were kindly greeted by Mr. Jonathan Olson, the director of the funeral home. He expressed his deep condolences and informed us of Claire's "condition" so we would be prepared to see her.

"As you know, the car hit directly on the passenger side of the car, exactly where Claire was sitting. Because of this, she is very bruised and has many cuts. You will notice that she has a deep cut on her neck. This cut is from the seatbelt. She has been cleaned up and I have no hesitations in letting you all see her."

He rose from his desk and proceeded out the door and down the stairs to where Claire was. We all followed. My dad held mom's hand and my aunt held mine. After we got to the last step, I hesitated to step further and turn because I knew that she would be right there. I heard my parents approach her body. My mom started to cry and continued to say "Oh Claire, my baby." Then after a couple of minutes, she said, "It's ok Laura, you can come in. Daddy and I are here for you."

I looked at my aunt, squeezed her hand, and preceded forward. There she was, lying on a cold metal table. She was covered with a sheet from her chest down. I felt her hand: cold as ice. I looked at her face, bruised and cut from glass. I went to the other side of the table to be close to my parents only to be disgusted from how painful she looked. To me, the deep cut seemed deeper than the Grand Canyon and represented nothing but the pain and misery she must have felt. What if they were wrong? What if she didn't die instantly? I forced myself to look away and to return to the other side, away from the deep cut.

"Are you ok Laura? You can stand over here with us."

"No Daddy, I don't like that side."

My dad looked at the funeral director and asked how we were going to cover up the deep cut.

"Typically we suggest putting on a turtle neck or a collared sweater. It would be your choice what you wanted to do. Any more questions? If not, I will leave and give you time with Claire. Take as much time as you need and if you need me, please do not hesitate to come upstairs."

Knowing that this would be our last time alone as a family, we spent what seemed to be hours down in that basement. We held Claire's hand, kissed her forehead, and I scooped down to hug her cold body. I whispered in her ear that I loved her, that she was the best sister ever, and that I would never forget her. My aunt and uncle came into say goodbyes and then we all went upstairs to re-join Mr. Olson. We discussed funeral arrangements, casket prices, and picked out an obituary card picture and a little saying. Mom and Dad kept including me in the decision-making process. I de-cided that Claire would really like the obituary card that had the white dove on it. Mom picked out a famous prayer for the front of the card. We went into the casket room. I sized up the choices. Some were cheap looking and all I could imagine was how bugs and worms would seep through on Claire and that scared me. Then I saw the beautiful wooden casket. It was dark wood with a light tan fabric inside. I hate to say that a coffin seemed perfect for Claire, but this casket did. It seemed safe. It looked like it would keep her warm. I didn't want her cold. I didn't want water to enter it. This was the one, and I'm pretty sure that my parents were thinking the same thing.

Mr. Olson looked at us and calmly said, "I know this is really difficult but I want you to know upfront that this is our most ex-pensive casket, but if it is what you want, we can make some kind of arrangement."

I wanted to scream! This was the last thing I was going to be able to do for Claire. All I wanted was a safe resting place for her and now Mr. Funeral director was informing us that we might not be able to afford it. The nerve! My dad's voice interrupted my angry thoughts.

"We bought life insurance years ago for both of our girls, and if I am correct, we'll be getting some kind of auto insurance money. We want the best for our Claire, and this is the one we want. We will be able to afford it, somehow."

When we got home, I immediately went up to my room. Seeing Claire had been so difficult and I preferred not to be around people. I needed to cry and decided that it was better not to cry in front of everyone. I shut my door and locked it to ensure I could be alone, but before I knew it, someone was knocking.

"Who is it?"

"Aunt Christine. Are you ok? Gavin is here to see you. I'm going to send him up, ok."

I didn't even respond. I didn't want anyone to see me like this and furthermore, no one knew how I was feeling. How many teens lose a sibling? I sure didn't know anyone. I heard another knock and figured it was Gavin. Sure enough, I soon heard Gavin's voice clearly asking if he could come in. I went to the door and unlocked it. Gavin opened the door and immediately gave me the longest hug I have ever been given. I started to cry into his shoulder and I continue to cry until I could cry no longer. We sat down on my bed and he put his arm around my shoulder. I didn't say anything and neither did he, and yet, I felt more comforted now than I had from anyone else since Claire died. At that moment I knew that no matter what, Gavin would be there for me during this really hard time. After some time, my aunt Christine returned to my room to tell me that Abby, Maddie, and Grace were here to see me. With that, Gavin left to go home but promised he'd come over tomorrow and that I should call if I wanted to talk. Nice offer but very unlikely that I'd call him.

Maddie and Grace came up to my room with Abby slowly trudging behind carrying my backpack and small overnight bag. They all gave me a hug, and Maddie started to cry. They kept repeating that they were so sorry and that they'd be there for me. They were my best friends and I truly believed that they would be there for me every step of the way. We didn't really talk, mainly because none of us knew what to say, but we sat there together for an hour. Having them there was a comfort in a time that I felt I could never be comforted.

Later that day Reverend Jacobs approached me about helping plan for the funeral.

"Laura, I think that it would be important for you to be involved in planning Claire's funeral. You were one of the closest people to her and because of that, you would have some idea of what she would want."

To be honest, I was tired of people saying what Claire would want because in my mind I could only see Claire wanting one thing: to be alive. Why would any 17-year old want certain songs or scriptures at their funeral? I'm sure she didn't care one bit. Why would she, she's dead! The funeral is more a closing for everyone else rather than an actual going away party for the dead person. Regardless, I agreed that I would look for scripture to be read, a decision my parents supported.

That night I sat down on my bed and opened my Bible. How was I supposed to find the perfect scripture for Claire's funeral? Claire was always someone who was strong in her faith and I knew her favorite scripture was from the book of Joshua. It sounded funeral appropriate to me, but then of course, how much did I know? Reverend Jacobs suggested one gospel reading and a Psalm, so I started looking for those. I started skimming Matthew, Mark, and Luke but didn't find something that was just perfect. Finally, I found something in John, chapter 14 to be exact.

I had been looking through the Bible for around three hours and had found two solid scriptural readings. I actually found this to be somewhat calming because I knew that I was somehow contributing to my sister's life, or I guess in this sense, the end of it. I decided to continue looking through the Psalms and finally settled on a Psalm from chapter 49. With that, I went to bed knowing that in two short days, those scriptures would be read at Claire's funeral.

Today was October 6, 2008, the day I would bury my sister. I didn't sleep at all the night before and part of it was because the upstairs felt so empty and sad that it almost hurt to be there. I took a shower and opened my closet to inspect my options. What does someone wear to their sister's funeral? Black obviously, but all black? I was feeling so sick from crying, lack of sleep, and barely eating in four days that I decided not to wear anything too uncomfortable. To be totally honest, I would be willing to go in my sweatpants and t-shirt if I knew my parents would be ok with it, but I decided not to ask. I put on a pair of jeans, which I thought was a nice compromise, and the black sweater that Claire bought for me last Christmas.

The only thing harder than picking out my clothes for this fateful day was helping my parents pick out Claire's final clothing, the clothes everyone would say goodbye to her in, the clothes she would wear for all of eternity, in the cold ground, forever. We had picked them after going to the funeral home once everyone had left for the evening. It was so eerie going through Claire's drawers and closet. My mom kept crying with every suggestion that my dad or I had. I mentioned that maybe Claire would like her soft-ball shirt, but Dad quickly rejected that idea because he thought we should keep it to remember her and anyways, "it wasn't appro-priate to wear a turtleneck under a t-shirt."

The whole turtleneck thing turned out to be more of a hassle than anyone could have imagined. It was definitely necessary because we didn't want everyone to see the gash in her neck, but Claire never wore turtlenecks and it would just look out of place. Then I suggested her favorite pair of jeans and my mom commented on how she wanted Claire to look nicer than just blue jeans. Despite her initial thoughts, she eventually decided on jeans because it would have been what Claire wanted. Claire always wore jeans which helped contribute to her down to earth persona. Then it was back to the shirt problem. Before we knew it, it was two in the morning and we still hadn't come to a decision. My mom was still crying intermittently, and I would be lying if I said I wasn't holding back tears. My dad finally found a nice sweater that would look nice with a turtleneck, but we still weren't done: what would be in the coffin with Claire? I knew that Claire would have wanted her softball glove and her Bible, but part of me was being selfish. I wanted those things to remember her by, especially her Bible. I was always so impressed with Claire's dedication to her faith. Her Bible's tattered pages and yellow highlights were signs of how much she read it. For some reason, I felt like her Bible was filled with deep insight or knowledge into life and that if I read it, I would somehow know more about her thoughts and beliefs about scriptural passages.

We entered the church at eight a.m. The casket was already placed at the front of the church and was ready for the visitation that would occur from nine until eleven. I hadn't seen Claire since the day at the funeral home and part of me was scared about walking up to say my final goodbye. My parents were in the entry talking with Pastor Jacobs, so I decided to take the opportunity to go see Claire, alone. I walked down the aisle and with every step, I knew I was getting closer to seeing the reality of my life. I could see the beautiful wooden coffin that we had selected. It may pricey but it was the right decision. Finally, I was there, but my eyes were closed, tightly closed, and my stomach felt as if the acid was churning to the point of explosion. I finally opened my eyes and there she was. The first thing I noticed was that her hair was not parted in its normal place and it bugged me, greatly. I touched her hand and was taken aback by how cold she felt. She was holding a softball and one of our family Bibles, a great compromise which allowed me to keep her glove and Bible to remember her by. Her blue sweater looked very nice and even the white turtleneck was pulled off, but that hair was really bugging me. It needed to be fixed before anyone saw her. I was angry. We had given the funeral home people a picture of Claire so they could make her look like herself and yet, the part was so far off! I went to get my mom so I could show her the hair issue. She didn't seem to think it was as big of a deal as I did, but knowing how much it upset me, she talked to the morticians and asked them if they could fix it. As they worked on the hair, I stood right next to them so I could coach them on where it should be located.

People started to arrive at quarter to nine. I tried to talk with as many as I could so that they knew we were grateful for their support and the love that they had shown Claire while she was here. Although I couldn't name everyone I talked to, I could clearly state the main points that were continually re-iterated to me. First, Claire was such a great and loving person. Agreed. Secondly, the drunk deserved to go to jail for a long time. Definitely agreed. Thirdly, it is your responsibility now to take care of your parents, you need to be strong for them now. Confusing, not agreed. How am I supposed to take care of my parents? Of course, I would be there for them and they will be there for me, but what does "taking care of them" require? It sounded like they were saying that I needed to move on from Claire's death so that I can focus on helping my parents. How could they say such things? How could I simply move on and be strong enough to get my parents through this? Regardless, I knew it must be true because why would so many people tell me that if it wasn't true? I decided that I would do my best to be strong. I would stop hiding out in my room to cry and instead, be really supportive of Mom and Dad. Maybe I'd help out around the house more and give Mom a break by making most of the meals. I could do that. Everyone counted on me to do that, so I must.

Soon it was eleven o'clock and my entire family of aunts, uncles, cousins, grandparents, and parents were ushered out into the entrance. I started to hear the sound of the organ and we began to walk into the church. I caught my breath as I immediately noticed the casket was closed. Claire was gone. It was ok, I would open it at the end when everyone left so I could say goodbye once more. I looked at my aunt and whispered about the casket being closed and that was when she informed me that it had been locked and sealed. I felt panicky as I realized it could never be opened again. Claire was trapped in that thing forever. I had been maintaining my composure fairly well up until that moment, but then I lost it and I felt like everyone was staring at me. I sat down next to my mom and dad. Everything around me seemed to be non-existent and I was quickly awoken from my unconscious when I heard Reverend Jacobs say, "Claire's sister Laura would like to share some of her special memories of Claire."

That was my cue. I shakily rose from my pew and stepped forward to the microphone stand. I cleared my throat, wiped the tears that were streaming down my face, looked over at Claire's closed coffin, and thought, this is it, I need to make Claire proud.

"Five years ago, my family gathered to say goodbye to my grandma, Josie. Although I knew I was going to experience further deaths throughout my life, I never expected that someone who was so young and that I was closest to, would be next. So today, we again gather to say goodbye and to celebrate the life of my sister, Claire.

I want to start off by reading Claire's obituary. Claire Ann Russell was born on April 22, 1991, at Jefferson County Hospital to James and Julie Russell. Claire died on October 2, 2008. Claire was a senior and honor student at Richard's High. During her short time here on earth, Claire made quite a difference in the lives of all of those around her. She was the starting pitcher on the varsity softball team, the secretary of the senior class, a dedicated worker at Countryside Nursing Home, a mentor to an elementary student, and a loveable and caring friend to everyone she knew. Claire had recently decided on applying to college in hopes of becoming a social worker who advocated for kids in foster care.

She is survived by her parents, James and Julie, sister, Laura, Grandpas Lawrence and Arnold, Grandma Gina, Uncle Robert (Carol), Uncle Eli (Donna), and Aunt Christine (William), cousins Brent, Bryan, and Derek, and countless numbers of friends.

This is what is printed in all the newspapers about Claire's life, but it doesn't say anything deeper than the basics, and I want to go beyond the basics and talk honestly about my sister, Claire. Like normal sisters, Claire and I had a fair share of disagreements and fights, but she has always been my best friend."

My voice started to crack as tears began to flow down my face. I looked over to Claire's beautiful wooden casket. I knew Claire was gone but I wanted her to be proud of me, proud of the fact that I was able to share deep intimate moments that I had had with her. I wanted to make sure everyone knew how amazing my sister was. After regaining composure, I looked up to at least a thousand people all staring at me. I continued.

"Claire and I have always been close and I have always looked up to her. When I think of our childhood years together, I am happily reminded of hours upon hours of playing with dolls, watching our favorite television shows together, and having milk drinking contests. I distinctly remember when I was around five and Claire seven, drinking milk as fast as we could. Claire finished first and made a funny face which caused milk to fly out of my nose and mouth. As we got older, Claire started to become interested in sports and rather than ignoring her younger, un-athletic sister, Claire always asked me to play catch with her and even spent countless weekends helping me to learn, not because she was desperate to find someone to play with, but because she wanted to spend time with me just like I did with her.

Claire continued to be the best sister anyone could ask for well into her teen years. When Claire got her driver's license, I was really afraid that she wouldn't want to spend time with me, but the exact opposite happened. She decided to have weekly "sister dates" with me. Every week we spent an afternoon or evening together, and Claire would drive us to the movies, bowling, a restaurant, or the mall. Our last sister date was two days before she died. We went to get ice cream. I got cookies and cream and she had a peanut butter cup. Ironically, our next sister date was scheduled for today. We had planned on going to the movies.

I will always remember Claire for her shining personality, kindness, humor, and great advice. Although Claire and I had our fair share of arguments, like all siblings, I always loved her and I know she always loved me. I will always miss the random text messages she would send for the sole purpose of saying hi or good luck on a test. Claire was a great person, a great friend, and a great sister. I know that God truly blessed me with a great sister, and although the 15 years we spent together were far too short, I await the day when I will see her in Heaven."

I looked around to my parents who were obviously impressed that I had the strength to get in front of everyone and say such memorable things about Claire. As I left the front and proceeded to take my seat back by my parents, I looked once more at the closed casket now displaying on top the vivacious senior picture of Claire. All I could think of was how that casket didn't contain Claire. That casket held a cold, pale, dead body, but not Claire.

Before I knew it, the service was done and to be honest, I don't really remember what happened. I know scripture was read and famous hymns were sung, but otherwise, nothing. I've heard that your mind protects you from things that are too hard to experience, and I think this was one of those moments. We all stood and the casket was pushed down the center aisle with my family following. It was placed in the hearse, and my family got into our car to follow. A line of maybe fifty cars followed the procession and concluded our trip at Maple Grove cemetery. Claire's pallbearers picked up the casket and rested it on the platform. Our pastor said some words and then it was all over. We headed back to church for the post-funeral lunch prepared by the women of the church. People around me were trying to coax me into eating, but needless to say, I didn't. My appetite was gone and I had no interest in going on a search to find it. My life seemed over as if nothing else really mattered. School didn't matter. All that future stuff like college didn't matter. All I could imagine was feeling this putrid feeling for the rest of my life. If this is how life would be from now on, then life definitely didn't matter.

CHAPTER THREE

I emailed Abby to find out more about what I was missing in school. The funeral was three days ago, and I still had no intention on heading back to school. I didn't want to and I felt like school was pointless. Why be educated if I'm going to die anyway? It didn't make any sense to me. There were still people coming over to our place on a daily basis, but I tended to stay to myself. Not that I was rude, but when I was downstairs with everyone, it was mainly to show my thankfulness for them being there for my parents, but I didn't feel support from the over-crowdedness of my house. Gavin had called last night and asked if he could come over today and hang out. I, of course, said yes because I do need a break from the stress of my life. I'm still not eating much which I think is a concern of my dad, but I just can't get myself to eat. Last night he came up to my room to have a father-daughter talk. The premise behind it was how much he loved me and how we were going to get through this and be a strong family. He encouraged me to talk about how I was feeling and then laid it on me that he was a little concerned with how I have been locking myself up in my room and not eating or sleeping. I appreciated his concern, but I can't say how I'm really feeling because if I did, I wouldn't be taking care of him and Mom like the people at the funeral told me to. They both have enough on their plate than to worry about me and the fact that I feel utterly hopeless and in actuality, lifeless.

It was around five that evening that I saw Gavin walking towards our house, so I went outside to meet him. I haven't really been outside of my room much less the house in a while, so I thought it would be good for me to get some fresh air. Before I could even say hi, Gavin gave me a big hug and held me for a long time. There was something about Gavin hugs that were so genuine and caring as if my life didn't suck as much as I felt it did.

"How are you doing Laura?"

I explained that I was doing pretty good and that I was looking forward to getting back to school. I said that I finally had my appetite back and that I was sleeping really well. He gave me that disapproving look. Gavin knows me so well that he can tell when I'm lying. Seeing his reaction caused me to take back what I said.

"I'm sorry Gavin. It is just so hard for me to talk about how I'm really feeling. To be honest, I feel awful. I'm not eating. I'm not sleeping. I don't care about school. My mom is always crying and I don't know what to do."

I started to cry myself. I think I needed to. I tried so hard not to cry in front of my parents because yet again, I didn't want them to have to worry about me, but with Gavin, it was different. I knew I could cry in front of Gavin. He stood up unexpectedly and went inside my house. A minute later he returned and explained that he told my parents that we were going to hang out at his place. He grabbed my hands to help me stand up from the ground and we walked over to his place, his arm around my shoulder the whole time. When we reached his house, I discovered that his parents were still at work which I was happy about. Gavin's parents are like my second parents and I didn't really want to have to explain how I'm feeling to them either.

"So, what do you want to eat? I could order a pizza. We could just eat a gallon of ice cream. I have peanut butter cookies, your favorite!"

"That's all very enticing Gavin, but seriously, I'm not hungry."

"Laura, you need to eat, even if it is just a little. If I ordered a pizza, would you try to eat some?" I agreed that I would, so Gavin called to place the order.

"Laura, you know you can tell me anything, right? And you know that I really care about you and that you are one of my best friends."

I knew that every word he said was true. Gavin was one of those people who was always there for others, especially me. We've known each other since we were little and I've always been able to tell him anything, but this, this was different because I knew without a doubt that Gavin had no clue what I was going through; in fact, Gavin has never had to say goodbye to even a grandparent or a pet. How could someone who has never lost anything have any encouraging words for me? So instead of talking about my bottled up emotions that were overtaking my being, I sat there and simply stared at the floor. I had no idea what to say, so I immediately changed the subject.

"How's biology these days? What are you talking about now?"

I think Gavin got my subtle hint that I didn't feel like talking so he kindly accepted my question and began to explain all about Mr. Thompson's lecture on neurons and how it had been so confusing. Before we knew it, the doorbell rang signifying that the pizza was finally here. Gavin went to the door and brought back the large pepperoni pizza. When I saw it, my stomach dropped. Yuck. The smell itself almost made me want to vomit. I looked at Gavin and gave him the "I'm not sure about this anymore" look, but instead of understanding, he grabbed a slice, put it on a plate, handed it to me, and said, "You promised." I took the plate and proceeded to take a bite. To my surprise, it actually tasted good, so I continued until I had finished the slice and decided to take another.

I looked at the clock. It was already eight, and I knew I should be heading back home. I thanked Gavin for the pizza and the company. He gave me yet another hug and promised to stop by to see me tomorrow.

When I got home, I checked my email. Still nothing from Abby which was really odd because she was usually an obsessive email checker, so I decided to call her. No answer. That was really strange, but maybe she was busy with some family thing. I had to remember that some people were still living their lives even if I wasn't. Regardless, I was tired, so I took a shower and went to bed.

The sounds of sirens surrounded me. I looked around and there I saw Kyle's car. "Claire! Claire! It's Laura, I'm here!" I ran to the car and saw Claire. She had a huge smile on her face. "I'll be ok Laura. Look, I'm not even scratched." I felt relieved. She looked so happy. All of a sudden she got an angry bitter look on her face. "Remember that fight we had this morning. Well, this is punishment." With that, Claire drew her last breath. "No!!!!" I woke up dripping with sweat. It was just a nightmare, but it felt so real. I looked at the clock. Two a.m. I knew I wasn't going to fall back to sleep after that, so I turned on my computer to listen to music and I didn't move an inch all night long.

The next morning I found myself taking another shower mainly to wake myself up but also because of the excessive sweating problem I had had because of the nightmare. I went downstairs and found my mom and dad sitting at the kitchen table.

"Laura honey, come have some breakfast with us."

"Sorry Mom, but I'm just not hungry."

Both Mom and Dad gave me the concerned look which went against the "no worried parents" policy, so I went to sit down with them. I poured myself some juice and had some toast and fresh fruit.

"Laura, your mother and I were discussing that you will need to get back to school next Monday. It is going to be very difficult, but we need to try to keep our lives as normal as possible. I'm even going to start back up at work next Monday."

My dad was a middle school science teacher, that's probably where my love of science originates from, so I understood why he would need to be heading back to work. I noticed that Dad didn't mention Mom getting back to work, so full of concern, I asked, "What about you Mom? When are you going to be going back to work?"

Mom explained that she would be taking some time off before heading back to work at Jefferson County Hospital. My mom is a nurse there in the maternity ward. My guess is that she didn't feel like she could go back to the hospital yet because the hospital is the one place where you are constantly reminded that there is something called death and it occurs every day. Furthermore, Alex Smith, the idiot drunk driver that killed my sister, was still there. If I were Mom and had to return to work in the same place that was caring for my daughter's killer, I think I'd maybe slip the guy some drug in his IV. Yeah, probably not a good idea for Mom to go back to work. Kyle was also at the hospital. He had just been moved from critical condition to fair. He's alert and conscious, just in a lot of pain, both physical and emotional. He can't believe that Claire is gone, well, no one can right now, but we at least saw her body, Kyle didn't. He had been unconscious and doctors didn't know when he'd become alert, so although we wanted to wait for Kyle to be out of the hospital, we couldn't put off Claire's funeral because we didn't know when that would be. I broke out of my personal thoughts and returned to the conversation with my dad.

"I'm not sure I'll be ready to go back to school Dad, maybe one more week off would be good for me."

Most kids try to get out of school, but I was serious. I didn't think that right now I could deal with the emotions and pressure of being back at school, surrounded by people who would constantly look at me as the girl whose sister died. How was I even supposed to keep up with my school work? My level of concentration was non-existent and all I ever felt like doing was laying around and thinking about how angry and sad I felt. Maybe school would distract me, but I imagined it would only add to my stress and thus wouldn't help one bit. Regardless of how I felt, my parents disagreed and said I needed to head back to school on Monday.

The day proceeded like all the other days since Claire died. People came over carrying various foods, the mailbox was filled with tens of sympathy cards, the Kleenex boxes went through their daily emptying, and there I sat in my room for most of the day. Gavin stopped by after school let out. He brought me a peanut butter cookie from Harvest Bakery because he knew they were my favorite and well, he had made it his new goal to entice me to eat food. It was nice of him but to be honest, it was kind of annoying to know someone is observing the food that I eat. He couldn't stay long, but he told me about school and how everyone missed me. I said I would be going back on Monday and then it instantly hit me, how would I get to school? I actually started to cry. Claire always drove me to school and I wasn't crying because now I wouldn't have a ride, but I was crying because it will be a million little things like that to remind me that she was gone, truly gone, forever. Gavin gave me a concerned look and put his arm around my shoulder.

"I'm sorry Gavin. I promise that I never really cry except for when I'm around you."

"Well, I do have that impact on girls."

He gave me a little smirk and I couldn't help but burst out laughing. I explained the whole driving to school thing and he offered for his parents to take me. It didn't sound all that bad because I would be arriving with Gavin who could definitely help with the transition process back into school. Besides, it was better than riding the bus or walking three miles. Also, I didn't want to bother my parents by asking for a ride, so I gratefully accepted. We sat there for about another twenty minutes, but Gavin had to leave because his family was going out to celebrate his Grandpa's birthday.

That night I went to bed a little leary because of the night before. I fervently prayed that I would not have another nightmare and I went off to sleep. The sounds of sirens surrounded me. I looked around and there I saw Kyle's car. "Claire! Claire! It's Laura, I'm here!" I ran to the car and saw Claire. She had a huge smile on her face. "I'll be ok Laura. Look, I'm not even scratched." I felt relieved. She looked so happy. All of a sudden she got an angry bitter look on her face. "Remember that fight we had this morning. Well, this is punishment." With that, Claire drew her last breath. "No!!!!" I woke up again covered with sweat. Then I started to cry and I was instantly filled with fear.

The days continued to pass, filled with sleepless nights which caused extreme headaches and the inability to function or even a desire to function. I still wasn't eating except for when my parents would have obviously noticed or when Gavin would entice me with food he knew I liked. Soon, it was time for me to go back to school. The thought made me sick. I wanted to crawl into a ball and just momentarily disappear. I was so afraid of what people would say or if they would look at me differently. I didn't want their pity but I knew it would happen. What if my friends treated me differently? I was afraid that they already had. Gavin, of course, hadn't changed, but Abby never called me back and returned my email only when I sent another. Grace and Maddie hadn't really talked to me since the funeral except for one or two text messages to say hi and that they missed me. Drew didn't talk to me at all. I didn't feel like they deserted me or anything, just that they didn't know what to say or how to react. I guess I don't blame them because I wouldn't know what to do in their situation either. I went to bed that night fearing the worst and hoping for the best.

I didn't sleep at all that night for a couple of reasons. First, I was so terrified that I would have a nightmare that I wouldn't let myself go to sleep and secondly, I was hoping that if I looked awful the next morning that my parents would agree that I should stay home from school. My six a.m. alarm went off and I got up to take my shower. Afterward, I went downstairs and found my parents sitting at the table with Tofty snuggling at their feet.

"Mom, Dad, I really am not feeling great. I think I should stay home from school one more day. Will you call the school and get me excused?"

They both looked at each other, probably both hoping that the other would step up and say no, but neither wanting to because they both wanted to appease the only child they had left. Finally, my dad cleared his throat and explained that I had to go back to school and the longer I put it off, the harder it would be.

"Laura, Claire would want you to continue on with your life. You need to go to school, learn, and see your friends. You're going to find that your friends will be your main source of support. Sure your mom and I are here for you, but you're not always going to want to talk to us, but your friends, they'll be there for you."

I gave him a slight smile to show that I understood even though it didn't make me happy. I went to the cupboard and grabbed a granola bar for the road.

"Is that all you're going to have?"

As kindly as I could, I said, "I'll be ok Mom. Seriously. I always ate a granola bar before and it never bothered you then." With that, I was out the door.

It's strange the little things that cause you extreme pain. The fact that Gavin's parents were driving me to school was yet another subtle reminder that my life was different. Claire would no longer be driving me to school, which in itself wasn't a big deal, but it was just another little thing to remind me that she was gone and that I wouldn't be spending time with her anymore. When we reached school, all I could do was look the window and stare at the obstacle in front of me. I knew Gavin sensed my hesitation but didn't want to say anything in front of his parents.

"Have a good day you two. And Laura, it'll be ok. Remember that we are always here for you, and Gavin will be here at school if you need someone to talk to."

Mr. and Mrs. Frost gave me a kind smile, and I opened the door and stepped out into the world, which I hadn't seen in what seemed like ages. The last time I was here, life was perfect, but now, my life is different, completely different, and it was all for the worse. Gavin stood beside me and patted my back.

"I know this is going to be hard Laura, but I'm right here." I gave him a little smile and with that, we walked into school.

Some people kindly approached me in the hall to welcome me back while others stood back not quite knowing how to react. When I reached my locker I found that it was covered in "Thinking of You" and "We love you" cards and notes. I did feel loved and I felt that people really cared, and yet, I didn't want to be there. It seemed wrong to continue on with my life when I knew that Claire would never be continuing with hers.

The first day was a sort of a blur. I was trying to find out what I was missing in every class, but some teachers were being more difficult than others. Not that they were mean, but they wouldn't give me a straight answer, but more of a "don't worry about getting it done until you're ready to do this." Nice, but stupid! I would never feel up to it, but if I didn't do it now, I would fall even more behind. I was finally able to coax them to give me all of my assignments and in doing so, I felt utter hopelessness. There was no way I could catch up in every class while still keeping up with the current stuff too. I had missed two papers, two quizzes, three tests, and hundreds of pages of reading. I felt like giving up right then and there. Luckily, Gavin said he was willing to help me catch up after school until I was completely caught up. In my mind catching up was impossible, but Gavin seemed to think that by the end of the week I could be caught up. I was able to convince my teachers to let me take quizzes and tests at home as long as I promised to abide by the strict time limit and of course, not use my notes or book. That would at least help some.

Math was the one subject that I always struggled with and I was afraid I would never be able to catch up. Luckily, that evening Gavin spent three hours helping me with my math homework. I knew I would be able to catch up on biology with no problem and I had already decided to use online reading summaries of my English book so that I didn't have to actually read it. I knew that was kind of like cheating or at least taking the easy way out, but I didn't care.

That night after I got home from Gavin's place, I found my mom sitting in the living room crying. My dad had apparently run to the grocery store which left my mother alone in her thoughts which was just too much for her to handle. I sat down next to her and gave her a hug.

"Are you doing ok Mom?"

All she could do was give a nod. It looked like she had been crying for hours, and the fact that the garbage can next to her was filled with Kleenex definitely supported my hypothesis. I felt awful for my mom and yet I didn't know what to say. What could I say that would help a grieving mother feel comforted? Why didn't the people at the funeral tell me that one? To be honest, they probably didn't know either, but it all goes back to that question of how I am supposed to be there for my parents, especially if I don't know how to help myself. Without talking, I simply sat there with my mom with my arm around her. I think at one point I mumbled that we were going to make it through this, which sounded comforting even though I didn't truly believe it.

That night I went to bed feeling a multitude of emotions: anger at Alex Smith, the idiot drunk who was still in the hospital, sadness that I was never going to see Claire again, confusion as to why God let this happen to our family, how I could support my parents, and guilt that Claire and I had had a fight earlier that morning. My life would never be good again, and right now, I felt like I was never going to be happy again. How could I be happy when such a big part of my life was taken away from me? Part of me hoped that maybe, just maybe, Claire would come back, as if this was all a dream. Well, a nightmare, but I'm just waiting for the day I wake up and my life is back to normal. I sometimes imagined what it would be like. I envisioned myself waking up and going downstairs, but before I was completely down the stairs, I would hear Claire's voice and her contagious laugh. When I heard it, I would run down the stairs and I see her sitting with Mom and Dad. That's when Claire would say "Good morning little sister!" Wow, what a perfect, non-existent dream, but I can still hope for it.

The next day I made up my biology test during my study hall. Science has always been my best subject, but this test didn't make any sense to me. I had to read every question multiple times before I even understood what it was asking. I couldn't even concentrate on it. When I turned it into Mr. Thompson, he asked how I thought it went. I almost cried because I, of course, knew I failed it. I have never failed any test, quiz, or paper, and have never come close in science. Regardless, it was complete and I was now one step closer to catching up in my classes.

I grabbed my lunch and went to sit by my lunch crew. When I sat down, I felt that something was different and it took me the entire lunch hour to figure out what it was. Abby, Grace, Maddie, and Drew didn't know how to act in front of me. Could they be happy? Should they ask me how I'm doing? If they did ask, would they prefer me to talk or say that everything was going ok? As far as I was concerned the bell couldn't come soon enough. I felt Gavin nudge me and then he looked down at his tray, which I, of course, recognized that he wanted me to look at mine. I was so busy taking in the awkwardness of the meal that I had forgotten that food was in front of me. Thanks for pointing that out Gavin, as if I actually did want to eat.

"I'm going up for dessert, Laura, want me to grab you something?"

He is just too smooth and I don't understand why he is so concerned about my eating, but a peanut butter cookie did sound really good.

"Actually, I'll take a cookie. Thanks Gavin."

With that, he left, which left me fully immersed in the awkwardness. Finally, I chimed in and was wondering if anyone had plans for the upcoming weekend. Abby enthusiastically replied that she was excited about Grace's sleepover. Grace shot Abby an evil look immediately.

"I'm sorry Laura, I didn't think you'd want to come with well, everything going on, so I didn't invite you. You are welcome to come if you want though."

I was hurt that I wasn't even invited, but even if I had, I wouldn't have gone, so I replied no. So that was it, not only did my best friend die, but my friends were going to be strange around me and leave me out of stuff. I wanted to cry but then Gavin returned with my cookie. I didn't even say peanut butter, and yet, he knew. It's strange that something as stupid as a cookie could bring me momentary happiness. Finally, the bell rang.

That evening I went over to Gavin's house for math help. After a couple of hours, we had had enough equations, variables, and jumble mumble.

"Gavin, did you notice that lunch felt different today?"

"In what way?" he questioned.

"Grace, Abby, Maddie, and Drew are all different. I'm different. I don't feel like I belong."

"Yeah, I noticed that everything seemed more solemn and serious but it'll change Laura. They just don't know what to say or how to support and comfort you."

"But you haven't changed Gavin, so why would they act so different?"

"Laura, I have known you forever, I care about you, and nothing that happens is going to change my friendship with you."

I was sitting in biology and realized that it just wasn't as interesting as it once was. Strike that, it was still interesting but I just didn't care anymore. Instead of daydreaming about science, I was daydreaming about spending time with Claire; in fact, some days I was actually sound asleep and dreaming about being with Claire. Sleep still wasn't coming easily so I figured I should take advantage of the rare spouts of sleep I could find. At the end of class, Mr. Thompson asked if I could stay after class, and I knew immediately what it was about. Once all the other students had left, I quickly commented that I knew he wanted to talk to me because I had failed my test.

"Yes, Laura, you did fail your test. You got twenty percent

. I understand that you're going through a lot right now, so this test grade is not a big concern for me, but what is a concern is your lack of interest in everything. You are falling asleep in class and when you're awake, I get the feeling that you are not paying attention. Could I see your notebook?"

I felt embarrassed because I knew that if I showed him my notebook, it would confirm his beliefs. Rather than being filled with notes on cells, it was filled with intertwined circles, crisscrossed lines, and millions of stars.

He sensed my hesitation and continued, "Laura, have you talked to Mr. Collins our guidance counselor? I think that you may find it helpful to talk about how you are feeling. This is a lot for someone your age to go through. I hope you will strongly consider it. I do hope that you begin to pay attention in class, but do know that I am always here to help you catch up on material that you either missed or don't fully understand. I am giving you back your test and I want you to take it home and make the corrections for half credit."

"Thanks Mr. Thompson." I quietly took my test and went off to lunch.

CHAPTER FOUR

That night as I lay sleepless I came to a comforting and realistic idea. The Bible is filled with stories of God testing the faith of people, so why couldn't God be testing my faith? He is capable of all things, so why couldn't He bring Claire back? That's right, God will bring Claire back. I just have to be patient and be an amazing Christian. I won't question why Claire died because maybe, just maybe, if I am good enough, she will come back. I can't believe I figured that one out. I wonder how long I have to be good. One week, two, a month, surely not longer than a month, right? For sure I knew I couldn't tell anyone this because they wouldn't believe me for a second. I looked at the clock. Two-thirty a.m. I knew I could fall asleep now because it would only be a short time until my life was back to normal.

The next morning I went into Claire's room to see if some miraculous occurrence had happened during the night, but all I found was an empty un-made bed. The fact that Claire did not make her bed still sat uneasily in me. She always made her bed and the only reason I could imagine that she didn't that morning was that I had been so mean to her. I proceeded to look around her room and decided to open her nightstand drawer. In the drawer, I discovered three journals, her current one which I knew had a beautiful fall scene on the front, and her two past journals. The three journals spanned her entire high school years. Claire was a devoted journal writer, something that I never really understood, but she seemed to take some strange pleasure in writing about her life, but for all I know, she didn't write about her life at all, maybe she wrote poems or stories. That sounds more like Claire. She wasn't the type to write about the weather and every intricate detail of her day. I knew that there was one way to find out and that was to open her journal, but I just couldn't, especially if she was going to come back. Imagine explaining that one... "So, I never opened your journals to spy on you while you were alive, but the second you died I ran into your room to investigate your life. And now you are miraculously back and I know everything about the past four years of your life." Nope, that wasn't going to happen. I placed the journals back in the nightstand and went to get ready for school.

I went downstairs for breakfast to find that my dad had already left for work and my mom was just sitting in the living room looking sadder than I had ever seen her.

"Hi Mom, are you ok?" She didn't even seem to hear me. "Mom. Are you ok?" Still no response. I walked closer and touched her back. She responded with a startled jump.

"Laura, please don't sneak up on me like that. You scared me."

"I said Mom twice and you didn't hear me. Are you ok? I can stay home with you today."

"No, you need to go to school. I am just fine. See, smiling. That means I'm happy."

I didn't believe her and she knew it. She looked rough. Her hair wasn't combed, she was in her pajamas, and she had dark circles around her eyes. I hadn't seen her like this yet. As I walked over to Gavin's to catch a ride, I was trying to figure out what to do. Do I call Dad? Should I talk to Gavin's mom and ask her to go check on my mom? Should I just let her be? What would the funeral "support your parents" people tell me to do? Maybe I could call my aunt and she could call Mom to talk. Maybe I should be the one to support my mom rather than relying on other people.

That thought made me feel deep guilt. I've been so focused on getting myself through this while still maintaining decent grades and trying to keep up with friends, that maybe I haven't been very supportive of my parents. Is that my job though? Sure to be supportive because that is what families are for, but should I be the main support for my parents? Should I be the one to get them through it and see the good in life? I doubted it, mainly because I myself could not see the good in life. Rather than talking to anyone about my mom's condition, I kept it to myself and rode to school in silence.

After the first hour bell, I was walking to my locker and I saw Kyle. It was his first day back to school and I wasn't expecting to see him. He wasn't looking good both physically and emotionally. His left arm is broken and the fact that he was walking pretty slowly led me to believe that he was still pretty sore. He looked like he hadn't slept in days. He saw me and looked as if he didn't know what to do. Should he wave? Should he come to talk to me? Would talking to me be too hard for him? Would it be too hard for me? I decided to walk to his locker to see how he was doing, but before I reached him, he quickly turned and went into the boy's bathroom. Although talking to him would've been hard for me, I did want to know how he was doing.

Again, I found myself not caring about my classes and drawing pictures of hearts, bubbles, and zigzags all over my notebook pages. My stats for the day were as follows: a C on an English paper, which I expected because it was supposed to be 5 pages long but I only wrote 3, a C on my biology make-up test, a pity B- on a history test that I truly deserved a D, and a call to the principal's office. As I entered Mr. Evans office, I also noticed Mr. Collins sitting patiently.

Mr. Evans, the principal, started by saying, "Laura, Mr. Collins and I wanted to meet with you because we recognize how difficult of a time this must be for you. We understand that in addition to grieving you are faced with trying to keep up with school, friends, and family, and that would be overwhelming for anyone, but especially a teenage girl. We are here to offer support and think you would benefit from meeting with Mr. Collins to discuss your thoughts surrounding Claire and schoolwork."

Mr. Collins interrupted by saying, "Laura, we are all concerned for you and want you to have a safe outlet that you can express your feelings."

Express my feelings to these people? I barely knew them. If I am unwilling to open up to my parents, my friends, or other family members, why on earth would I talk to a strange man I barely knew? I had no interest in telling Mr. Collins my feelings about how I believe Claire will come back. I don't want to talk about my nightmares or my disgust for food. I don't want to tell anyone about how I feel responsible for caring for my parents or how that last interaction I had with Claire had been me yelling at her. No one understands so why would I want to talk to them. Although I felt like crying, I decided to lie by saying, "Actually, I've been able to talk a lot with my Aunt Christine and that has been really helpful, so I don't think I need to talk about my feelings. Thank you for your concern, but I should be getting back to class." With that, I stood up and left without looking back.

After school, I started preparing dinner for my parents. It was just spaghetti but it seemed helpful nonetheless. I also vacuumed, scrubbed the toilet, and tidied up the living room. I was doing my best to take care of my parents and to be a good person. Seriously, I have this thing under control and I'm sure that after a few weeks of this, Claire will be back and life will be normal.

Two weeks later I realized that I was delusional to ever believe that Claire's death was just a nightmare and that if I was a good person, she would return. I continually cried myself to sleep over that revelation. She'd been gone over a month now and yet, life was still chaotic and unpredictable. My friends had become more like themselves and yet, I felt like I didn't fit in anymore.

While they were busy gossiping about boys, clothes, and makeup, I was absorbed in grief and not knowing how to help my parents. My grades were still down and I had no desire to work to get them back up. I imagined that if I decided to go to college that I could simply explain why they were low, so there was no need to try.

At lunch on Friday, I talked to Gavin before the other four made it to the table.

"Gavin, are you free this weekend? Although I don't feel like getting out and doing something, I really need to try to have some fun. I don't fit in with Abby, Grace, and Maddie anymore, and I just really need you now."

I was almost in tears because it was true. I honestly felt so alone and it hurt even more to know how clueless my best girl-friends were. None of them had asked me how I was doing or invited me to hang out since the funeral. I'm not sure if it was because their lives were normal and happy and they didn't want a depressed girl bringing them down or if they just had no clue how much I was hurting. I imagined it was some of both. Gavin just looked at me with his caring eyes, as if wanting to scoop me up and hold me until I stopped feeling pain. That was when I realized that I truly loved Gavin Frost, that is in a friend way. I love being around him. I loved how whenever I'm with him that he makes me forget some of the sadness.

Drawing me away from my thoughts, Gavin finally spoke. "Laura, I'd love to do something with you this weekend. Let's make a whole day of it. I'll take care of the planning and you don't have to do a thing except to smile. You deserve a break."

With that, I felt at ease. Spending all Saturday with Gavin would be a great escape from my sadness. Just then Abby, Maddie, Grace, and Drew showed up. We started our small talk about our day and then Gavin asked what they were all doing this weekend. Turns out that on Saturday all the girls were going shopping.

"Oh and Laura, if you want, you can come too," Maddie said.

"No thanks, Gavin and I are going to hang out tomorrow."

With that, the bell rang but as everyone was getting up to go, Abby stopped me. "Hey Laura, I know we haven't been hanging out much since, well you know, but way to go with Gavin. I guess you must be over Drew, so I was hoping I could maybe ask him out on a date since you like Gavin now."

It all started to fall into place. Maybe Abby was starting to slip away because she was interested in Drew Harris, the boy I've had a crush on for two years and she wanted to snatch him up before I could. To be honest, Claire's death has really shown me who my true friends are. First, there is Gavin who had been there through it all. He has been a shoulder to cry on, a friend to laugh with, someone to get me peanut butter cookies, and the person who helped catch me up with all of my homework. Then there was Abby, Maddie, and Grace, who rarely talked to me and never asked me to hang out. And finally Drew, the boy I dreamed of dating who hasn't supported me in any way. He's never asked how I am doing, offered any help, and didn't even show up to Claire's funeral. When you put it that way it was easy to answer Abby's question, "Yes Abby, I am over Drew. Good luck asking him out."

I was laying in bed on a bright and sunny Saturday morning when I heard the doorbell ring. I looked at the clock. Six a.m! What is going on? I open my bedroom door to peek out and see my mom, who is still in her pajamas, greeting Gavin.

"Hi Gavin, what are you doing here so early?"

"Sorry to bother you so early Mrs. Russell, but I promised Laura that I'd plan an all-day fun day and although I'm sure she didn't expect me here this early, I am ready to take her to Big Al's for pancakes."

I started to walk down the stairs, and my mom turned to see

me and gave me the "you take care of this" look and she went back to bed.

"Gavin, this is not what I expected when you said you were planning a fun day. It is six in the morning and a girl needs her beauty sleep."

He laughed a little and said, "Laura, you don't need beauty sleep, you always look good to me."

I punched his shoulder and said, "Haha. Someone's trying to be funny." I grabbed his arm, brought him inside, and closed the door. "I'm just going to go take a shower and get ready. It'll take me less than twenty minutes but feel free to turn on the tv." With that, I ran upstairs and got ready for the day.

We were sitting at Tony's Pizzeria for lunch. Wow, it was only one in the afternoon and we had already had pancakes at Big Al's, walked around the city lake, and played Frisbee at the park.

"So what's on the agenda for the rest of the day Mr. all-day planner." Gavin looked up from his greasy cheese pizza with a smile and said, "Wouldn't you like to know."

After lunch, Gavin took me to the mall to play air hockey at the arcade. It wouldn't have been my first choice for fun but playing with Gavin definitely made it better. After the arcade, Gavin said he had a surprise back at his house. When we got to his house, it was already past six meaning our all-day fun day had already lasted twelve hours and yet, there was more. Gavin took me to the kitchen and handed me a recipe card.

"Seriously, we're going to bake peanut butter cookies! This day keeps getting better and better."

Gavin smiled and said, "Not only are we going to make them, but we are going to devour them as we watch a movie."

After the cookie baking, we settled in the family room to

watch a movie Gavin had picked out. Thankfully, he decided on a comedy because despite all the fun we've had, I didn't want to watch a drama or sad death story. He popped in the DVD and then sat down on the couch next to me and then without hesitation, put his arm around me. Although he's done that before, this felt different because it wasn't out of comforting me but rather wanting to be close to me and to be honest, I wanted to be close to him too. I scooted closer and rested my head on his chest. Maybe Abby was right, maybe I truly have fallen for Gavin Frost, the boy next door.

At the end of the movie, I randomly started crying. I wasn't really sure why, but to be honest, I think I was sad that I couldn't go home and tell Claire about how Gavin had put his arm around me and had planned this day-long date just for us.

Gavin's concerned eyes looked at me. "Why are you crying?"

"I'm so sorry Gavin. Today has been wonderful and I've had such an amazing time with you but for some reason, I just started missing Claire."

He hugged me tighter and put his head down on mine. "Hey, I have an idea. Why don't you tell me some things you used to do with Claire? What are some of your favorite memories?"

"Won't that make it worse by talking about her?"

"Laura, you need to think about the good times, not the bad ones, so tell me all about the good times you and Claire had together."

With that, I spilled everything. I talked about how Claire and I used to go to the mall, get ice cream, and cry together during romantic movies. I told Gavin about the time we went on a family camping trip and Claire and I used to compete to see who could roast the best marshmallow. I continued to talk for what seemed for hours and Gavin just said there and listened. "Thanks Gavin, that really did help."

He smiled, "It was good to hear more about Claire too. You know, maybe it would help if you wrote down your memories in like a journal so that you never forget all the great things you and Claire did together."

With that, I realized that maybe it was time to crack open Claire's journal now that I know she's never coming back. Maybe it was time to discover Claire.

CHAPTER FIVE

Early Sunday morning I walked down the hall to Claire's room. Although she's gone, I still feel out of place going through her things, and I don't want my parents to know. I opened her nightstand and I saw her journals. I carefully took them and went back to my room. As I sat in bed staring at the three journals, I contemplated whether to actually read them. What would I find? What if it said something bad like how she never liked me and that I was annoying? I started to second guess my decision, but curiosity got the best of me.

I opened up the first journal labeled "Freshman year." The first entry was from September 6, 2005.

"I can't believe I'm already a freshman in high school! Although I'm a little nervous about what to expect, I am excited to begin. I have so many things I want to do in high school: play softball (I'm hoping to make the varsity team as a freshman), be part of the Little Buddies program, maybe try some art classes, and decide what to do with my life. I have so many things I want to accomplish in my life and since I'm getting older, I should make a list so that I can start accomplishing them.

1) Go to a foreign country
2) Volunteer for a summer
3) Save someone's life
4) Get married
5) Adopt a child
6) Write a message in a bottle and throw it in the ocean
7) Write a book and publish it

8) Learn how to sew a quilt
9) Befriend an unlikely person

Now for some ridiculous things I'd like to accomplish

10) Learn how to say "Hi" in 10 different languages
11) Sleep on a deserted beach
12) Eat a gallon of ice cream in one sitting with my future husband

I closed the journal. Claire had amazing dreams and maybe, just maybe, I could live them out for her. I got dressed and went to talk to Gavin. I needed to show him Claire's dreams and maybe, the two of us could accomplish them.

Five months later... April 2009

It came, it finally came. I held my letter from Towering Pines Camp. It took me over a month to convince my parents to let me spend the next summer volunteering at a camp for children whose siblings had disabilities or illnesses. Gavin, on the other hand, didn't need to convince his parents, but I've grown used to the parental overprotectiveness that losing a sister brings.

"Mom, Dad, I got the letter from Towering Pines Camp. They accepted me as a full-time volunteer!" My parents were excited for me but I could see in my mom's eye that she was slightly nervous. "Don't worry mom, the camp is only forty-five minutes away. I plan on coming home every weekend and don't forget, Gavin will be there with me."

A slight smile curled up on her face, "Laura, I'm so happy for you. Despite how rough the past seven months have been, you've really done well. Your grades are starting to go back up, you're starting to spend more time with your activities, and you have Gavin. Oh, Laura, Gavin is such a great boy and I know you will both have a good time volunteering. I'm just so happy you have something you can look forward to."

"Thanks, Mom. I love you. Now I'm going to go check with Gavin to see if he got his letter."

As I ran over to Gavin's house, I realized just how much has changed in my life. In the past year, I went from being a normal girl who was slightly nervous about being a high school student to the only person at my school who has lost a sibling. I battled depression and if I'm completely honest, it still feels like it comes and goes. Three months after losing Claire I started to eat normally and the fifteen pounds that I had lost slowly started to return even though I wish it hadn't. At one point I was failing every class but now my grades are all up to C's and B's which is significantly lower than my typical straight A's, but for what I've been through, I'll take it. To be completely honest, every day was still a struggle. A struggle to get up, get dressed, do my best at school, act interested in my friend's stable lives, and to try to take care of my parents.

I knocked on Gavin's door and as he opened it, I threw my arms around him.

"I guess you got your letter too," he said.

"Sure did. What is your assignment for the summer?"

Gavin explained that he'll be working as a lifeguard, which we had both expected since he is certified. I, on the other hand, will be a junior counselor meaning I, along with the senior counselor, will be responsible for the safety of eight to ten girls.

"Sounds like a lot of responsibility, doesn't it Gavin?"

He laughed, "As if keeping your eyes open for drowning kids isn't a lot of responsibility." I punched him in the arm and together we went downstairs to watch television.

Two weeks later was the day I had been dreading for months, Claire's birthday. People had told me that the first year would be the hardest because you go through all of the firsts without the person: the holidays, birthdays, and family vacations which all lead up to the first death anniversary. The people who said that were right. Thanksgiving and Christmas had been so difficult this year. All of my aunts, uncles, cousins, and grandparents tried to make it a happy occasion for us so that we could forget our grief but instead, we all started crying by the end of the night. But today, Wednesday, April 22, 2009, was another one of those difficult days because it was Claire's 18th birthday. I wasn't sure how to act today, especially around my parents. Should I show how obviously sad I am that this would be Claire's big 18th birthday or should I not bring it up in hopes that they magically forgot? I went downstairs to have some breakfast only to find my mom crying on the couch while my dad had his arm around her. I guess they didn't forget. Be strong. Be strong. I walked up to my parents and tried to hold back the tears.

"I love you guys. Don't worry, we'll get through this."

My mom looked up at me with a little smile and grabbed my arms to hug me. "Oh Laura, do you know how much you mean to us? We love you so much. Please always be careful. We can't lose you too."

I tried to reassure them that they'd never lose me, but we have all become too aware that nothing in life is ever certain.

I was riding in the car with Gavin to school. Thank goodness he finally got his license a month ago because it meant more free-dom for both of us. I had started to think about whom among my friends would remember this difficult day. Surely Gavin would, right? I didn't think my other friends will and even if they did, I doubted they would even mention it. We pulled up the Richard's High and surprisingly, Gavin hadn't mentioned anything about Claire's birthday.

At lunch, I sat staring blankly into space while Maddie, Abby, Drew, and Grace chatted about who knows what. Like me, Gavin just sat there quietly and listened to the conversation. As the bell rang, I stood to throw away my trash and Gavin quickly followed.

"Laura, wait up. Something is not right today but I can't figure it out. Why are you so out of it?"

I completely lost it and began to cry like a small girl who couldn't find her mother. "You forgot Gavin. Out of all of my friends, I thought for sure you'd remember."

Just then it must have clicked because those beautiful deep eyes filled with regret and sadness.

"I'm so sorry Laura. I'm an idiot. I had remembered last week and then it just slipped my mind. Tell you what, let's just get out of here. We can call our parents and get excused." A half an hour later, we were on the road, and I was incredibly thankful for Gavin and for understanding parents.

That was an afternoon I will never forget. Gavin and I went back to his house to watch a movie. As I snuggled up beside him, he cleared his throat and said, "Laura, I'm not sure if this is the best time to do this, but with this past year being crazy and all, I'm not sure any time will be perfect. I was thinking that maybe this day should hold a special event in addition to Claire's birth-day so that it doesn't always feel so sad. You know that you mean the world to me and I truly care about you and I think you feel the same. Will you be my girlfriend?" I looked up at him with a smile, shook my head yes, and then Gavin kissed me for the first time.

CHAPTER SIX

Journal entry:

I'm trying to narrow down my career path. I'm thinking teacher, social worker, or occupational therapist. In other words, a helping career. I know I want to have a job in which I make a difference and I specifically want to work with kids. My dad is a teacher and he loves it and I think having summers off would be nice, especially when I have kids. Being a social worker could be fun too because they work in so many settings like schools, hospitals, and community organizations. It just seems like I'd have the opportunity to try new areas. Occupational therapy sounds neat too because you're helping kids after accidents or who were born with a disability.

When I was in middle school, there was a boy named Carl who had Down Syndrome. He was funny and nice. Everyone loved him which was nice because I know that not all kids with disabilities are accepted and loved by classmates. I also remember that Carl was adopted. I'm not sure if his biological parents couldn't provide for a child with a disability or if he would've been adopted even if he was typically developing. Regardless, I want to make sure that every child feels wanted and accepted. Maybe I should be a social worker and help kids in the foster care system.

CHAPTER SEVEN

Summer had finally come. Claire had been gone for over eight months now and I was just starting my quest to discover more about her by completing her life goals. I packed my bags with all the essentials: swimming suit, sunscreen, hat, bug spray, and flashlight, and then I loaded everything into Gavin's car. My mom stood nervously at the door as she watched me load my things. I could see her holding back tears which made me feel like I wasn't doing my job of protecting them but this was something I had to do, both for myself and for Claire.

I hadn't told my parents about the list for a few reasons. First off, I think they'd want to read through Claire's journals to find hope and meaning, like myself, but I doubted they were emotionally healthy enough for that. Secondly, they'd tell me I was crazy and that I needed to follow my own dreams, not Claire's. For all I know, maybe they were right. Maybe living out Claire's dreams will only delay my breakdown. What if I don't find what I'm looking for? For goodness sakes, what am I looking for? What will I feel when the list is complete? I put those thoughts aside and walk towards my parents.

"Remember to wear sunscreen," my mom said tearfully.

"Mom, I will be fine. This will be a good experience for me to help people and will take my mind off of Claire for a little while. You said it yourself, I need things to look forward to and this is one of them. I'll be home next weekend and we can do something together. Maybe we could go shopping or get our nails done, just you and me."

She showed a hint of a smile and said, "Okay, I'll get us an appointment." Dad patted me on the back and looked to Gavin as if to say, "Watch out for her."

When we said goodbye to Gavin's parents it was much less of an ordeal. No tears, no sadness, just goodbye, we love you, be careful, and have fun. I sometimes wondered if my parents would be more like Gavin's if Claire were still alive or if there would still be a hint of nervousness.

As we left the driveway, I looked back and saw my mom in tears. I felt so guilty for causing even more pain, so much so, that I started tearing up also.

"Hey, cheer up. This is going to be a great summer!"

"I know Gavin but still, I feel so guilty for leaving my parents alone. I feel like I'm really letting them down."

He looked over at me with that "I'm sorry everything is so hard" face but then quickly turned it into a joke by saying, "At least we know Tofty won't leave them too." I started laughing and realized just how true it was, they have our beautiful golden retriever to keep them company along with countless family and friends.

We were pleasantly greeted at Towering Pines Camp by about twenty various coworkers. Some were older and must have been program directors while others were close to our age. They all seemed so enthusiastic that it was almost overwhelming. As they introduced themselves, they helped us move all of our belongings to the staff training cabins. By the end of the move, I had already met Madison, Emmie, Will, and two Chloe's, one of which has decided to go by Sully since her last name is Sullivan.

The cabin was filled with ten sets of bunk beds, which although they were currently filled with the staff's belongings, would soon be filled by many excited little girls. The bunks were old metal bunks with thin, plastic-covered mattresses. Although they didn't look comfortable, I put the thought aside and focused on my mission: live out this dream for Claire and hopefully learn something along the way.

Madison turned and smiled at me as she put my backpack on the lower bunk, "It's not much, but it'll be home for the next two and a half months. By the way, I'll be the senior counselor working with you this summer, so I'm sure we'll get to know each other really well!"

I smiled but deep down I was slightly nervous because Madison looked very similar to Claire. She was around the same height, weight, and hairstyle. Also, she, like Claire, may be the only girl I know who pulls off the athletic look while still managing to attract hundreds of interested boys. I brushed aside my initial nerves and decided that I wouldn't let them get to me.

I came to know more about Madison as the days passed. She was eighteen years old and had just graduated from high school. Imagine that, even more in common with Claire. One difference became clear, Madison planned on going to college for math, something Claire never would've considered.

I also learned more about my fellow co-workers. Camp leaders encouraged all staff to share their hopes and fears for the summer and even life, especially because the kids we were working with were coming to camp with their fair share of fears. It hadn't fully hit me that I was going to work with kids who have had to navigate the emotional toll road of having a sick sibling but I felt that losing Claire somewhat helped. At one of our sessions, we each described one secret we were hiding from the group. Sully was the first to talk and she described that her mom had battled cancer on and off for three years, and despite currently being in remission, she was always anxiously awaiting to find out if it would return again. Emmie then discussed that she has battled with anorexia for the past five years. Madison said that she went to this camp as a kid because her younger brother, Elias, has Down syndrome. I intently listened to story after story and then it was finally my turn. I knew what I had to say simply because I still have very off days and those around me need to know why I could all of a sudden break down in tears. My voice was shaky at first but seemed to normalize after a few seconds. I described my past year in concise but clear details: my sister Claire died. I have no other siblings. I spent weeks hoping she'd magically return, and I still cry almost every day. With that, I started crying and felt incredibly embarrassed to have shared so much with people who are essentially strangers. Surprisingly, everyone surrounded me to give me a hug, and I felt embraced in love. The feeling was wonderful and yet strange. My friends from school, who had been my friends for several years never made me feel as comforted as these new friends at camp. Although I came to camp to fulfill Claire's dream, I realized then I would leave with much more.

Two weeks of training passed faster than I ever could have imagined. We practiced water emergency drills, learned about a variety of disabilities and illnesses that our camper's siblings face, were certified in first aid and CPR, played millions of camp games, and sang songs around the campfire. The weekend between our training I had spent at home with Mom and Dad. Mom and I went out to get our nails done and then did some shopping. I had realized that I had somewhat wrongly guessed what I would need for camp and let's be honest, I completely over packed. I swapped out my three heavy sweatshirts, two pairs of jeans, four capris, and eight t-shirts for one lightweight sweatshirt, one rain jacket, five athletic shorts, one pair of athletic pants, and a combination of t-shirts and tank tops. Mom seemed so happy to have me back at home, and I could tell that both she and Dad really missed me. While part of me felt really guilty that I left, a bigger part of me felt happy. Of course, not as happy as I once was but definitely happier than I had felt since Claire died and even overall happier than when Gavin asked me to be his girlfriend. I decided this summer was going to be perfect with new friends, bonding with

Gavin, and hopefully impacting the lives of numerous kids.

Finally, Madison and I received the list of names and pictures of each of our first-week campers. Madison held up a picture of a smiley ten-year-old girl with long brown hair.

"That's either Quinn or Nora. They both look so similar."

Madison started laughing. "Yes, they do look a lot alike but this is Nora."

Then she held up Quinn's picture so I could see the difference. Next was a girl with curly blonde hair and it was definitely Piper. Long auburn hair was Stella. And we continued until we had covered the rest of the girls: Brooklyn, Lucia, Maggie, and Violet. By the time the girls arrived, we would be able to recognize and call them all by name.

The next day the girls arrived. Madison and I heard the cabin door open and we quickly went to greet our first camper.

"Hi, Maggie! Welcome to camp."

Maggie and her parents both seemed pleasantly surprised that we welcomed her by name. We introduced ourselves and helped Maggie pick a bunk bed. Her parents soon left and more and more girls continued to arrive. Although we had seen their pictures, it was completely different to see them in person because we were able to see their personalities. From her picture, I would have assumed that Brooklyn was quiet but she was actually quite energetic and outgoing. On the other hand, I thought Nora would have been rambunctious but she was very shy, almost too shy.

We took the girls down by the dock to play get-to-know-you games, set cabin rules, and discuss the activities they wanted to do during the week. All the girls seemed to enjoy the games and were excited to participate in every camp activity, except Nora. They decided they wanted to roast marshmallows, take a night hike, and compete in a morning polar plunge. We determined a cabin name, wrote a chant to sing at group campfire, and went to have dinner at the lodge.

That evening we had a variety show where the staff did skits and sang songs around the campfire. Madison and I did a skit about butterflies that had the life lesson of including everyone. Of course, the kids clapped but there was no laughter until Will and Gavin did a skit about a monster named Frankie and his desire to eat everything in sight. All the cabins shared their names and chants, including our girls who decided on "Badger Bandits," being that they were all from Wisconsin.

After all of the cabin groups left, our girls stayed by the campfire to make s'mores. Amongst the burning of marshmallows, I found myself actually smiling and laughing. I didn't feel weighed down by my grief and for the first time in months, I didn't feel guilty for smiling. My happiness continued to peak as I heard my girls discussing the cute counselor who played Frankie because Frankie was played by my guy. My Gavin. In spite of my happiness, I became more aware that Nora still didn't seem happy. Perhaps this was more than being shy. Maybe she was homesick or actually sick. I couldn't tell but I decided that if she didn't seem better tomorrow that I would ask her.

That night I fell asleep and for the first time in nine months, I didn't have a bad dream. I hadn't told anyone, even Gavin, that my nights were still plagued by bad dreams although they weren't as scary as they once were. Nowadays they tended to involve spending time with Claire only to wake up and realize that she was truly dead. I woke up feeling refreshed and excited to start the day. I went with the girls to eat breakfast and was delightfully surprised to see my favorite, waffles with strawberries. The girls were passing around the orange juice and by the time the pitcher got to me, it was all gone. With that, my world felt like it was crashing and I felt dumb for thinking that my mere twelve hours of not feeling sad or having bad dreams was a sign that I was moving on. The empty pitcher was a reminder of the fight Claire and I had had on the day she died. Seriously, why did I ever get mad at her about orange juice anyway? Fighting about something so dumb and never apologizing was the biggest regret of my life. I really do still miss her and still can't fully comprehend what it truly means that she is dead. I also can't comprehend what it truly means that I will have to live the rest of my life without her.

"Laura, do you want me to go fill up the pitcher?"

I heard the words but didn't take them in. I hear the girls laughing and again Lucia asks, "Laura, are you daydreaming? Should I go get orange juice?" I laughed it off as feeling tired and agreed that they could go fill up the pitcher.

The day went well but I was still feeling a little down despite all the fun I was having. Throughout the day I played an exciting game of capture the flag, went swimming and canoeing with Madison and our girls, and had ice cream in the afternoon. Although I ran into Gavin on and off throughout the day, I was glad he didn't notice or comment on my mood because sometimes it is easier to just deal with it alone versus feeling that you have to talk about it.

That evening all of our girls opened up about their siblings. Violet started by saying, "My older brother is sixteen and he has a brain injury. He wasn't born with it but he was in an accident when he was thirteen. Sometimes he gets angry for no reason and other times he seems really sad and depressed. I was only seven when he was in the accident so it has been hard for me."

Piper spoke next. "My brother has a brain injury too, Violet. He is twelve and got his from sledding down a hill and hitting a tree when he was ten."

Madison spoke up by saying that maybe Violet and Piper should try to spend some extra time together this week to discuss their brothers since they both have an idea of what each other are going through.

Next to talk was Stella who described that her six-year-old sister has severe epilepsy. "It is always so scary because you don't know how long the seizure will last and I always worry that she won't wake up."

Quinn commented that her older brother, who was thirteen, has autism and he doesn't talk but sometimes will hit or bite himself when he can't communicate what he needs. The night went on with sharing. Brooklyn's younger brother had cerebral palsy, Lucia's older sister had spina bifida, and Maggie's little brother, who was adopted, had fetal alcohol syndrome. I anxiously waited to hear more about Nora's story. She spoke quietly and simply stated, "My twin brother Charlie has cancer."

Of course, I felt horrible for all the girls but having a sibling, especially a twin, with cancer must be really scary because you never know if it will spread or return following a remission. I think everyone agreed and began comforting Nora. Madison broke the silence by thanking everyone for being so honest.

"What about you guys? Tell us about your brothers and sisters," Violet said.

Madison started by saying that she was a camper here her whole life because her fifteen-year-old brother, Elias, has Down's syndrome. Then it was my turn to answer the dreaded question. What should I say? Should I explain that I have a sister but she died? Or should I say I am an only child? Or better yet, I could just say I have an older sister but that she doesn't have a disability. Of course, Madison knew the real truth but I figured there was no need to talk about death with young girls who have sick siblings, so I simply stated that I had an older sister, Claire, who was eighteen years old.

That night, the bad dreams returned but it was different than it had ever been. I was walking under a rainbow in an open prairie, and I heard Claire's voice as clear as can be. "Hey, little sis. It's me. I just wanted to say that I love you." I immediately woke up and was frightened and yet hopeful that in some way I had actually talked to Claire. The other dreams I had seemed so fake because her voice wasn't quite right, but this dream was different because the voice was just right. Each word sounded strong, clear, and yet cheerful, and I found myself imagining Claire feeling happy in Heaven.

The week continued to pass quickly. I felt that I had really grown attached to my girls but still felt that Nora was disconnected from the group. Thursday afternoon I took her aside and asked her if there was something she wanted to talk about.

"No, I'm fine."

I wasn't sure whether her response was completely honest, so I decided to press a little more. "What's been your favorite part of the week?"

She hesitated and then finally spoke up, "I loved our night hike on Monday night. It was wonderful to see the stars and learn more about the constellations."

I agreed that I enjoyed that part too but again, I felt uneasy from her response. "Nora, I just get the feeling that something is bothering you and I want you to know that you can talk to Madison or me about it. We're here to help all of you girls."

Nora looked at me and I could tell she was near tears. "Laura, has anyone you loved ever died?"

Hearing that word "died" hit me hard and I wasn't sure how to respond, so all I said was yes. Nora prompted by asking me who I had lost. I too started to tear up as I simply stated that the sister I had talked about, Claire, it was her who died. Nora started to fully cry and explained that she hadn't been fully open about her brother Charlie.

"Charlie died three months ago. I miss him every day. I didn't want to come to camp but my parents wanted me to. Sorry, I didn't say anything the other night but I just couldn't."

Losing Claire has been so hard for me but I couldn't imagine what it would feel like to lose your twin brother at the age of ten.

"I'm so sorry Nora. Do you want to talk about it?"

Nora began telling me all about her brother Charlie and as she spoke, I felt as if I was listening to someone much older and wiser than just ten years old.

"Charlie and I always did everything together. We played games together. We sat together on the school bus. He helped me with math and I helped him with reading. He wasn't just my brother but he was and still is my best friend. Charlie found out he had cancer when we were seven. He lost his hair and would get really sick after he had chemotherapy. He was always taller than me but cancer made him so sick that he started using a wheelchair so he looked shorter and younger than me. At one point he had been in the hospital for over a month and then he came home. I thought he came home because he was getting better, but he didn't. He died two weeks before our tenth birthday. That birthday was really sad, and Mom, Dad, and I cried all day. I will never forget when Mom and Dad told me that Charlie was with God and Grandma Betty. Mom and Dad said that Charlie was healthy and happy now but that I wouldn't see him anymore. For a long time, I was confused because I saw Charlie at his funeral and he just seemed asleep. One night I cried all night and asked Mom where Charlie was and she explained that the funeral was my time to say goodbye and that I won't see Charlie again. She said that though I can't see him, he is always around me and keeping me safe. Even though he is with me all the time, I still really miss him and wish he was here. I don't have any other brothers or sisters and none of my friends understand, so I feel alone."

Although I tried to hold myself together for Nora's sake, my eyes flooded with tears and my heart exploded in pain. Despite not being ten, I knew exactly what Nora felt: alone, confused, scared, and sad. It's a feeling that you can't explain to people who haven't experienced a significant loss. Even though I'm close to Gavin, I still know he doesn't understand what I go through, especially because he's an only child. As I looked at that sad ten-year-old face, I knew that we had something in common that few people our age do, and despite our age difference, we understood what it felt like to lose a sibling. I gave Nora a hug and told her that my big sister Claire was playing games with Charlie in Heaven, and I truly believed it. Claire loved children and I know that if she hadn't died, she would be preparing to enter college to get a degree in social work so that she could help kids in the foster care system.

I thanked Nora for sharing and for the next hour, we sat together to talk and cry. I told her some things about Claire, like how she was about to go to college, all the memories we shared during our sister dates, the things we did together as kids, and ultimately, that she passed away in a car accident. I felt that in some small way that I was helping Nora feel less alone in the world, and if I must admit, I myself, felt less alone too. I started to realize that even in times of sadness, I could still use my experiences to be a source of support for others. I decided right then and there to do everything I could to make sure she felt happy, even momentarily, during her final day of camp.

Later that day, I ran into Gavin. He held me tightly as I cried and relayed my whole experience with Nora.

"Gavin, I just don't understand why that sweet little girl has to go through such pain."

"Laura, I ask myself the same question. You are the best person I've ever met and you still are going through something imaginable. It's not fair, but I'll tell you one thing. Laura, you were meant to help Nora. It's almost like Claire meant for you to find that journal and helped send you here so that you could help Nora and other kids like her."

I smiled. The thought that Claire was with me while I pursue her dreams, made me realize my true dream: to be as adventurous, compassionate, and as giving as my big sister.

"Gavin, I have a plan."

I huddled by my girls that night at the campfire. It was slightly colder than usual, which helped with mosquitoes, but also left us with a slight chill. Violet and Brooklyn giggled on and on about Gavin; in fact, all the girls had all week. I almost wished I could have said "He's mine" just to shoot up a few more points on the cool stage. Just then, Gavin stood up to perform in a skit.

Gavin cleared his throat, "I'm going to need some special help from a camper for this skit."

With that, every hand in the audience shot straight up and I distinctly heard my girls enthusiastically yell "Pick me!" Gavin looked around for a second as if trying to make a decision. Then he pointed at Nora. She automatically blushed a little and stood up enthusiastically.

"She's so lucky," Piper said.

All the girls from the cabin agreed. Gavin took Nora to the side and whispered to her what to do. I could tell she was laughing a little from what Gavin was saying. Together they completed a skit about two kids on an adventure. During the adventure, Gavin pretended to fall into a pile of mud and got his hair all dirty. He asked Nora what he should use to wash it. She smiled and said "Mustard." With that, she squeezed real mustard into his hair and Gavin proceeded to attempt to wash his hair.

"Nora, that didn't work. Any better ideas?"

Nora laughed and grabbed a can of tomato soup out of Gavin's backpack. "My mom used this when my dog got sprayed by a skunk. Maybe it will work for you."

Gavin poured the tomato soup into his hair and kept scrubbing. Everyone was laughing so hard but Gavin kept a straight face.

"Nora," he said in a frustrated voice, "this isn't working!"

Again, Nora smiled and went to grab her final cure. "What about this shampoo? Unfortunately, I don't have any water."

Immediately Gavin took the shampoo, ran from the campfire, and jumped in the lake. He trudged back up the hill to the campfire and was completely soaked!

"Nora, it worked, my hair is clean."

Everyone clapped and cheered loudly. Gavin stopped the cheering to publicly thank his amazing assistant, Nora. Her smile shined and I knew that at that moment, she felt true happiness as any ten-year-old child should.

The next day Madison and I said goodbye to all of our girls. Although I bonded with all of them, saying goodbye to Nora was significantly harder than I could've imagined. When her parents came to the cabin, she started to cry and hugged me tightly. I knew just as well as she did that leaving camp meant returning to reality. It was the same feeling I felt when I returned home on weekends.

"Nora, we can still write letters to each other. Here, this is the camp address and the other one is my home address. Feel free to write me anytime you want. I'll be thinking of you but I know you'll be ok. We'll both be okay."

"Laura, do you promise it will get easier?"

All I could say was "Yes," even though I questioned it all the time.

The rest of the summer flew by and before I knew it, Gavin and I were packing up the car to leave Towering Pines Camp. I had received and responded to numerous letters from various campers, but I was always most excited to get a letter from Nora. Her last letter detailed that she and her parents had gone to Florida to visit family. She sent a picture of her by the ocean and although she was smiling, I could tell it was that fake smile that I saw at camp. Little did I know at the time, but her letters would continue to come for years and as time passed, I knew that I had truly changed this child's life.

CHAPTER EIGHT

Journal entry:

Today I went and donated blood because the school was sponsoring a blood drive. It took about ten pokes, but one of the nurses finally got a vein. She said I have small veins that kind of wiggle so they are hard to get. It took a little while to complete the donation but I just sat and thought about who might receive my blood. I can't believe how advanced modern medicine has become. Just think, I'm an average person and yet, even I am capable of saving someone's life. Someday I really hope to truly save someone's life, like maybe perform CPR or donate a kidney or bone marrow. I always hear stories on the news about a miraculous organ donation or how the right person was in the right place to save a life. In fact, I heard one of those stories yesterday on the news. A college student was walking home from a late night class and came across a young child with autism who had wandered from home. He called 911 immediately and officers said if he hadn't found the child, that he could have frozen in the frigid temperatures. What I love most about this story was that during the interview, the college kid said that he usually went home a different way; in fact, this was the first time he'd ever gone home that way but he felt he should. That's a miracle. That's what I dream of being a part of.

CHAPTER NINE

After returning home from camp, Gavin and I still had a couple of weeks before school started. It was a difficult transition from camp to home for many reasons but the main one was that I felt thrown back into the realization that my life wasn't what I wanted it to be. At camp, I was so focused on helping the kids that I was able to remove myself from my sadness and problems, but I forgot they were always waiting for me at home.

I laid on my bed and for the first time in many months, I let myself completely lose it. I cried, screamed, and punched my pillow as hard as I could. Tofty, who laid on the floor by my bed and observed my emotional tantrum, responded by licking my feet. The pain of losing Claire felt so raw, and I know deep down that I was regressing and I did. The bad dreams started to return, my appetite dwindled, and my motivation to do anything completely left. At night when I couldn't sleep, I would become engrossed with reading Claire's journal, something I had promised myself not to do. Seeing her goals was one thing, but reading her most personal and intimate thoughts was another, but I, unfortunately, hadn't followed through on that promise. The tears rolled down on the page as I read her every word. Claire's journal wasn't filled with gushy details but rather her thoughts and wisdom on the world. One thing I hadn't realized was that Claire wrote poems and oddly enough, whenever I read them, it felt like it fit my life.

The Wave (June 2009)

The waves approach the sand
While on the shore, my mind waits
To be touched by the calm
To be changed through its purity
My thoughts surround myself
As they expand into the distance
The wind carries off
My thoughts to the world
My mind seems lost in a universe
A universe not my own
As I dream of love and peace
The world infiltrates my mind
I wonder what will come and go
My mind ponders my dreams
Will peace come and hate go
Or will hate end the world
My mind is on the shore
Now surrounded by the sounds of thrashing
    waves
The furious thrashing waves
Reflect the uncertainty of our world

There were two other poems that seemed to impact my emotional state. Oddly enough, Claire wrote these poems within a month before she died.

The Question (August 2009)

There comes a time in everyone's life when they are faced with a question

A question so difficult that they could become two
different people depending on the direction they take

The question leaves you alone
You're surrounded by black
You can't see or hear but you feel the thumping of your
heart

Both directions have suns and clouds
Both directions have night and day
Both directions have pain and joy
Both directions have happiness and sorrow

You smile and you frown
You laugh and you cry
You search for help but you must do this alone
Despite the debate, you make a decision
Was it the right choice?
You may never know

Goodbye (September 2009)

A tear streams down your cherry colored face
        as a lump gathers in your throat
You see the nearing car
It's time to say goodbye
You turn to avoid the pain, if only for a minute
        to dream for something different
You feel an arm draped over your shoulder and

you feel less empty
You feel a connection
A love warming your soul
It says that it'll be okay
That you are not alone
The person soon embraces you in a hug
You find yourself wanting to walk away
but you unexpectedly turn to face the fear
To face the pain
You realize your strength
You are not alone
You are surrounded by love and messages
     of hope carried by the wind
Goodbye you whisper
Goodbye
Goodbye
Goodbye flows with the wind

Claire didn't say what the poem meant but to me, it seemed so sad and yet meaningful to my life. I am faced with the question of whether I am going to let Claire's death completely control my life or if I am going to continue my life and use my experience to make me a better person. Will I ever be able to say goodbye? Is Gavin the person who will always be there to help me face the pain? Simultaneously as I pondered that thought, the doorbell rang and I knew immediately that Claire had answered my question because to my surprise, I opened the door and saw Gavin standing there.

"Hey, Laura. I know it sounds silly, but I just felt like you needed me and the feeling must be correct because I can tell you've been crying."

No words needed to be said because seeing and hugging him

was all I needed to feel like I could get through this. Gavin's surprise visit also confirmed for me that my big sister was still watching out for me.

The next day I received a letter from Nora, and I felt reconfirmed that I still do have a purpose in this crazy life.

Laura,

Thanks for sending me your home address so I can keep writing even though camp is all done. I hope you had a good summer at Towering Pines. My summer turned out okay but I still really miss Charlie. Do you miss Claire? I feel like I have been missing Charlie even more lately because I've been so bored this summer. Charlie and I always used to spend our summers playing games and swimming, and now I have no one to that stuff with. School is starting soon but I'm not looking forward to it. Mom and Dad have set up playdates with some of my friends but we don't really have fun together anymore because I'm sad and don't want to play with them. My friends also treat me differently now. We used to have fun but now they are quiet and always make me pick what we do. I think they feel bad for me. Do your friends feel bad for you too?
Nora

I wrote Nora back immediately and confirmed her thoughts without adding too much emotion. At camp, I strived to remain a strong role model for her. Yes, I still miss Claire and it is okay for her to miss Charlie because we love them. Yes, my friends still feel bad for me and are different than before but it is important to still have fun with friends. I ended the letter by reminding Nora of how funny the skit she did with Gavin was. With that, I closed my eyes and asked Claire and Charlie to take care of little Nora.

The weekend before returning to school was Labor Day weekend and incidentally also my sixteenth birthday. While most six-teen-year-olds can't wait to get their license, I felt hesitant. Driving reminded me of Claire's accident which made driving scary for me. I was worried something could happen to me too and it just felt safer for me to wait until I was really ready. I figured that until then, I'd have Gavin around who could drive.

I've always been someone who looks forward to my birthday and enjoys celebrating, but this birthday was different because it was the first without Claire. My family is usually pretty low key with birthdays with my mom making our favorite foods and getting us a special dessert but this year my parents decided to go all out. I woke up early to the smell of my favorite breakfast, fresh homemade cinnamon rolls. My parents and I ate multiple rolls each and then my mom announced we were going on a girls day full of shopping and manicures and pedicures.

"Are you and Gavin still going out tonight," my mom questioned.

"Yeah, I think he's picking me up at six for dinner and a movie."

My mom mentioned that we should expand the girls day then to include a trip to the salon to get my hair done for my big date. It sounded like fun but all I could do was laugh.

"Mom, you know Gavin could care less what my hair looks like, and let's be honest, what can the salon do to tame these curls?"

Regardless of my thoughts, my mom said it was decided and called to schedule an appointment with Carla, our favorite hair stylist.

Spending the day with my mom was fun and refreshing. Sometimes it feels like we've both changed so much since Claire died, almost like we are totally different people. We're both reserved, quiet, and serious and let's admit it, two serious quiet people stuck together can be kind of depressing, but today, it felt differ-ent. I felt like we were reconnecting as mother and daughter. Our talks while our feet soaked at the spa seemed like they used to and we both found ourselves laughing. I talked about camp and how much I missed it. Mom talked about work, volunteering for the church fundraiser, and the weekend her and Dad spent visiting one of my great aunts. One thing led to another and then all of a sudden Mom was asking all about Gavin. I couldn't help but blush and giggle.

"You really like him, don't you?" I nodded that I did. "And he treats you well." Again, I nodded. "Laura, I know your only sixteen and you have your whole life ahead of you, but for some reason, I really feel like you and Gavin are meant to be together forever." All I could do was smile and hope my mom was right.

After our manicures and pedicures, we had lunch, got our hair done, and went shopping for some cute clothes for my date. I was surprised at how cute my hair turned out, and I was very excited when I found the perfect dress to wear that night. The dress was a knee length, single strap, green dress that would go perfectly with my dressy flats. I found a white shrug that worked perfectly with the dress.

Gavin arrived promptly at six. I opened the door and thought he was going to faint.

"Wow Laura, you look." He paused when he saw my dad look-ing on from the kitchen. I smiled and he mouthed the word beau-tiful. Gavin was wearing khaki shorts and a polo.

"You're not looking too shabby yourself," I laughed.

We had dinner at Francesco Pasta House and then watched the new Kevin Gray comedy. On the way home, Gavin stopped at the park and we sat by the lake and listened to the crickets.

"Ugh, I really am not ready to go back to school. This summer was so amazing and I don't want it to end."

Gavin agreed and then took my hand. "Laura, honestly, how are you doing?"

I took a deep breath and was about to say that I was fine, just missing camp but I know Gavin knows me so well that he already knows I'm struggling.

"Honestly, I'm having a hard time. Summer was an escape for me. A chance to help others and not think about my life. And now I'm back to normal life. At camp, I felt normal but here it seems like I'm known as the girl with the dead sister. My friends aren't really friends anymore. Teachers will still treat me like I'm breakable. At home, I still feel like I need to be strong and somehow get my parents through this, but I know I can't. You're my saving grace. What would I do without you?"

With that, he said, "You'll never have to find out." And then Gavin told me he loved me.

That night I wished I could tell Claire all about my evening with Gavin but I couldn't. I opened her journal to the time she and Kyle started dating. She had written about their special memories like first dates, first kiss, and there it was, the first I love you. The entry was dated June 2006.

"Tonight Kyle took me out to dinner for our six month anniversary. I wore my cute light blue dress and curled my hair. Kyle didn't tell me where we were going and I wish he had, because I was definitely overdressed. We drove to an open field on the outskirts of town and he revealed that he had packed a picnic meal for us but first we had to hike to his favorite spot in the town. We hiked for what seemed like miles, but it just felt that way because of my sandals. Then we came to a small pond and sat and talked while we watched the beautiful sunset. He talked about football and then he smiled and said he loved me. I just know we are going to get married someday."

Even though it makes no sense, I felt sad for Claire. I know what it's like to feel in love and understand that feeling that you've meant the one. The difference is that I still might marry my one and Claire never will. I know Kyle is going to be starting college this week. He still calls and stops by occasionally but I'm sure that will gradually fade to nothing. Honestly, I hope it does because Kyle is such a great guy that he deserves to move on and find someone else.

The first day back to school went well. One could call me a nerd, but I especially enjoyed my science classes, environmental science and physics. Unfortunately, I was still stuck having to take math, trigonometry, to be exact. Not sure how I'll survive it but I've definitely learned to put things into perspective. If I can survive a sister dying, math should be a cake walk.

At lunch, Gavin and I sat talking about what's next on the journal list.

"I think I'm going to learn how to sew a quilt. No clue how or who would teach me, but it could be fun."

"You know, my mom used to sew when I was little. I don't think she ever made a quilt, but she would make my Halloween costumes. Should I see if she could help you?"

"Gavin, that would be great. I'm thinking of making a tee shirt quilt of Claire's shirts and giving it to my mom for Christmas. That way even though Claire isn't making the quilt, she is still part of it."

Just then, Maddie, Grace, Drew, and Abby came and sat with us. They spent lunch talking about their summer breaks, vacations they took, and the parties they went to. Maddie, Grace, Abby, and Drew spent all summer together and Abby and Drew had actually started dating. Gavin and I talked about our experience at camp. It was quite obvious that we didn't fit in with the others. As we discussed comforting children who were dealing with sick siblings or in Nora's case, a sibling who died, they all just looked at me.

"Why would you want to do that? Aren't you depressed enough?" Drew asked and then looked as if he wished he could take it back. Not that I had been keeping track, but again, another instance why I'm glad I'm over Drew Harris.

I was kind of dumbfounded at the time but eventually said, "Sometimes helping others allows you to help yourself." I don't think they understood, but how could they? I wish I didn't understand either.

That night I was feeling down. Missing camp, missing how life was just a year ago. I opened up Claire's journal hoping for some encouragement, almost like a connection with her. Honestly, I don't know what I needed to hear at that moment but whatever it was, I didn't find it. Instead, I read an entry about when Claire got her license.

"Freedom, finally. I'm licensed to drive. Dad took me this morning for my test and I passed with flying colors. After my test, Dad took me out for lunch and had a big conversation about trust, honesty, safety, and responsibility. Of course, he already knew getting my license won't be an issue but it was like he felt like it was the dad thing to do. Then right as we were finishing up lunch he quickly added," one last rule, if a boy is ever in your car, the car becomes my car. "I couldn't tell if he was joking or not... I guess if I ever break that rule that I just have to make sure he doesn't find out. "

I closed the journal and let out a little laugh. Claire, a rebel, I think not. Claire was always the perfect kid. Maybe she was joking or maybe she had some spunk we never knew about. I turned off my light and prayed for restful sleep.

CHAPTER TEN

Journal entry:

I did something today that I never thought I'd do, skip school. It's crazy! I know that if twenty years from now I were to sit down and read this, I would have never believed that I actually did it. I'm a good girl. Reliable. Honest. Hard working. Definitely not the one to cut class but I did and if Mom and Dad found out, I'd be in trouble. So, about a month ago, Kyle told me that Lucas James was having a small radio-sponsored concert following the morning show and that he had won tickets by answering three trivia questions. He knew Lucas James was my favorite so he called every opportunity he could until he finally got through and won. Unfortunately, we both knew our parents wouldn't let us go, so we became "sick." We both set it up well and a few days before started to feel like we were "coming down with something." His parents would ask him if he was hanging out with me and he'd say he just wasn't feeling up to it and I said the same. That really meant we had to be sick. Then that morning, I pretended to throw up and boom, Mom called the school. She offered to stay home with me but I said no because I'd just sleep all day anyway. With everyone gone, Kyle came and picked me up and off we went. We planned on being home before our parent's lunch break, just in case they were to decide to check in us. It all went perfectly. No one knows and we had a great day. Lucas James was fantastic and he even autographed his CD for me.

CHAPTER ELEVEN

It was finally here. The day I've been dreading. Honestly, I still relive that day in my mind. I remember that clothes I wore, what I did, how I acted, and how I learned the bad news. I woke up praying that the day wouldn't plague me, and I tried to accept the fact that today was truly just another day of living without Claire versus clinging to the fact that today is the anniversary. But I couldn't. I felt ill. And not just a little upset stomach but that illness that hits deep in your stomach when you feel that something is not right. In other words, I was too sick for school so I didn't go.

I took my shower and went downstairs for breakfast. My mom and dad were having scrambled eggs and pancakes. They seemed OK but I'm guessing it was a show so as not to upset me. My mom had the day off too, so I declared, "I'm not going to school today. Mom, let's have a girl's day." My mom smiled as if to say thanks. I know she appreciates these bonding moments more than I know.

"I'll call the school and say you're not feeling the best today."

After Dad left for work, Mom and I planned out our day. Claire dying had really changed our relationship. We've both become more serious and we struggle to laugh and really enjoy our time together, or with anyone for that matter. I was determined to make today different. I miss the old days. I remember when Claire, Mom, and I had girl's day before. We would get lunch and not care if we ate too much and then we'd window shop for hours, get ice cream, and go to the movies. We'd laugh constantly and sing to the oldies blaring in the car. We didn't have a care in the world. I really missed those days.

Mom and I went to the mall to go dress shopping. Homecoming was in two weeks and I still hadn't picked out a dress for the dance. After trying on about ten, my mom found the perfect dress. It was a knee-length brilliant blue dress with a lace overlay.

"You look beautiful."

"Thanks, Mom."

During lunch, we talked about school, more adventures from summer camp, and mom's favorite topic, Gavin.

"He's just such a nice boy, Laura. I'm glad he treats you so well. I can tell he really cares about you."

I smiled, "He's pretty special."

We were leaving the mall and heading to Joe's Ice Cream shop. The music was on but we weren't singing, but rather silently enjoying each other's company. Mom slowly turned down the volume.

"Laura, I'm sorry the last year has been so crazy. I'm sorry Dad and I have been aloof. Things are so hard but never forget how much we love you!" She started to cry.

"Mom, there has never been a day in my life in which I questioned whether or not I am loved. You and Dad have always treated Claire and me well. This past year has sucked and I truly miss Claire every moment of every day, and although things feel different between us, I know I'm loved and I pray you know that I love you guys."

Mom pulled over the car at the nearest gas station and we sat and cried together. We talked about everything, missing Claire, not caring about school, and the never-ending feeling like my friends abandoned me. Mom talked about missing Claire, hating work, and feeling like she's missing out on seeing me grow up.

I'll never forget that day with my mom. We reconnected and in a way, felt partially healed because we had been able to fully confide in someone else. It was nice to feel that I could cry and be honest with her in a way that I've never been able to be with anyone else, even Gavin.

Two months later and approximately one hundred hours of hard work led to a beautiful t-shirt quilt. Gavin's mom, Kathleen, and I sat back and looked at the quilt we had finally made.

"Laura, it's beautiful and so special. I know your mom will absolutely love it."

I have to admit, it did look pretty good. My hand swept across it and took in each shirt. I had used shirts from Claire's softball team, church mission trips, her favorite professional sports teams, and the college shirt she got shortly before she died. I was even able to find two shirts from elementary school: one of a play she was in and one from an after-school club that had her name on it.

Gavin's mom was a natural at sewing. She understood the importance of interface and how to thread the bobbin just perfectly. I, on the other hand, learned how to push the fabric under the needle after she set everything up.

"Thanks, Mrs. Frost. I really appreciate all your help."

"Oh Laura, I've loved helping you and getting to know you better. Gavin talks about you all the time and I know he wants you in his life for years to come, so it's been nice spending all this time with you."

I smiled and tried to hide my giddiness. I obviously knew I was important to Gavin but maybe I didn't fully grasp the magnitude. It's nice to know that he feels the same way for me as I do him.

That night I wrapped the quilt up in beautiful Christmas wrapping paper and tied a ribbon with a bow on it. I usually don't go through such lengths with making a present look pretty, but this present was different.

Christmas morning came and my family gathered around the tree. This was the second Christmas without Claire and her absence still hurt. I remember when we were kids that we'd run downstairs bright and early to examine our gifts. We weren't allowed to even touch them until after breakfast. Mom would work hard to create the perfect Christmas breakfast of homemade cinnamon rolls, egg bake, and freshly squeezed orange juice. Now the rolls were replaced by store-bought muffins, the egg bake exchanged for frozen mini quiches, and freshly squeezed orange juice traded for a bottle of juice. I wasn't picky. It still tasted good, but yet again a reminder of how much things have changed and how unhappy these special occasions had become. After breakfast, we opened gifts.

"One gift left for you, Mom. It's from Claire and me."

My mom looked at me with a puzzled and almost saddened look. Was this all a mistake? She carefully removed the bow and ribbon and gently unwrapped the paper. She unfolded the blanket and began to sob.

"I didn't mean to make you cry, Mom. I thought this would be a special gift to remember Claire by."

"Laura, this is special. It's beautiful. This is the most thoughtful gift I've ever received. I'm just so taken aback. When did you learn to sew?"

I explained how I'd been working with Kathleen Frost and that she taught me some things but that she'd done most of it. My mother gave me a huge hug and simply said, "You will never realize just how much I love you."

Later that Christmas day, Gavin and I exchanged our gifts. I honestly struggled to come up with something meaningful for him but I eventually settled on an engraved pocket whistle that he could use year around when lifeguarding. I opened my gift from Gavin, a beautiful leather bound journal.

"To write of your adventures," he said. It was a perfect gift. I've never been much of a writer, but after reading Claire's journal, I started to think about the importance of documenting your thoughts and feelings, just in case something were to happen. Gavin then unwrapped his. "Thanks, Laura! This is perfect! I lost my last three whistles and now everyone will know this one is mine."

CHAPTER TWELVE

After Christmas break, I decided to join a service club. I hoped that giving back to the community would allow me to not only help others but also continue to feel like I have a purpose. I decided to join a group called Heroic Sisters, an organization which pairs high school girls with younger girls to serve as a strong role model. I completed a questionnaire about myself: likes, dislikes, and goals for my involvement. Two weeks later the guidance counselor, Mr. Collins, called me to his office.

"Laura, I know you're interested in the Heroic Sisters program and we have someone we think you'd match well with but you had written you preferred a younger child. The individual we have is thirteen but she has Down syndrome. I know she's older than expected but we recognized you to be a very reliable and respectful young adult and we think you'd be perfect for her."

I hadn't expected to be a heroic sister for a teenage girl but I was more than willing. "That sounds great!"

"Wonderful," Mr. Collins said. He handed me the girl's information so I could contact her mom and set up a get-together.

Later that night I read her profile. Her name was Rosie and she liked animals, particularly dogs, gardening with her mom, and reading books. I called her mom, Helen, and explained that Rosie and I were paired to be Heroic Sisters. She sounded elated that someone somewhat close in age would be spending time with Rosie.

"Usually she plays with much younger kids. Most girls Rosie's age are busy with boys, shopping, and makeup and Rosie just isn't at that stage yet." We planned to all meet at the library coffee-house on Saturday morning for smoothies and get to know you conversation.

Saturday came quickly and I must admit, I was feeling a little nervous. Although I worked all summer with siblings of kids with medical conditions like Down Syndrome, I've never actually been around sometime who had it. Would Rosie seem like a thirteen-year-old or would she seem younger?

I was shocked when I got to the coffee shop and meet her and her mom. Rosie definitely looked like a teenager and I was surprised her mom had mentioned that she wasn't into shopping because wow, she was one fashionable girl. She wore cute skinny jeans with adorable ballet flats and a beautiful blue sweater. I quickly glanced and my jeans and hoodie and made a mental note to try harder next time.

"Hi, I'm Laura."

Rosie and her mom both introduced themselves and after ordering our smoothies, we sat down to get to know each other. I found out that Rosie's parents are going through a divorce and that's been hard for her. She stays mostly with her mom but does see her dad occasionally on weekends. Rosie talked about their large sheepdog, Roxie, and I talked about Tofty. We made plans to get together again in a couple of weeks and see a movie together. Helen thanked me again and said how important it was for Rosie to have a friend.

The next week at school was crazy. I had multiple tests and research papers due so I was essentially busy every waking hour. Wednesday at lunch, Gavin talked the gang into going out Friday for dinner and a movie. Honestly, we haven't really done anything as a group since Claire died, meaning it's been over a year. It might be nice to start doing things together again, or maybe I'll realize it's time to move on.

Friday night Gavin and I met the gang for pizza. Abby and Drew were still dating and it seemed to be going well. They are both pretty into public displays of affection and I must admit that it's a little too much for me. Maybe Gavin and I are too modest in that sense, but that's more comfortable for us. Grace talked a lot about her older sister's upcoming wedding and how excited she is to be in the wedding. She continued to discuss all the details and then all of a sudden stopped and stared at me.

"I'm sorry Laura. I'll stop talking about this." I must have had a confused look on my face because she followed her comment with, "Well, with you not having a sister anymore, I thought maybe it might bother you for me to talk so much about mine."

I didn't know what to say or how to even respond. I wanted to say that I still do have a sister, but she's just not here. I wanted to say it didn't bother me one bit to hear about her sister's wedding and she was the one who made the situation sad by bringing up Claire. I wanted to say that they obviously didn't care about me and how I felt for a long time, so why bring it up now? I wanted to ask these things and before Claire's death, I never would've dreamed of saying anything, but now, now I didn't care. I was sick of being treated differently and thought of as being fragile. I was sick of being left out of things solely because they thought it might be too hard for me. I was sick of not having my life back. And I blew up.

"Do you guys realize this is the first time we've hung out since Claire died? You heard me right, the first time. I've been left out of everything because you're too afraid that somehow something will come up that will make me feel sad and that I'll bring down the fun group mentality. I've felt so abandoned and so friendless. I lost Claire and my best friends. I was so hopeful that tonight would be the start of a new relationship with us where we actually see each other outside of the lunchroom but maybe I was wrong. You guys treat me like I'm going to break and that I can't handle anything. Grace, of course, I want to hear about your sister's wedding because I care about you and what's going on in your life. I'm not going to all of a sudden breakdown and lose it. Please, I just want to be treated like a normal person. I don't want to be the sad girl with the dead sister anymore."

With that, I grabbed my purse and left. As I reached for the door, I heard Gavin running behind me to catch up.

"Laura, wait." I stood outside in the snowy air.

"Gavin, please don't ask if I'm ok. I'll never really be OK again, but I'm living and breathing and doing the best I can to find the good in life. I'm just so tired of not fitting in and I feel like no matter how hard I try, people are afraid to let me back in. They're afraid to hurt me and all I want to say is that I'm already hurt. Nothing is going to change that and nothing can make it worse. I always put on a smile even when I don't feel like it and yet, people will never treat me as normal again." I wanted to cry but I couldn't because the tears wouldn't come.

"So, the girl with a smile, what should we do now?"

I laughed. "Well, I guess I don't always put on a smile." With that, Gavin drove me home and we made plans to go to the movies tomorrow instead.

The next day, Gavin wanted to get to the movies early to "beat the rush." Considering the movie came out a month ago, I knew the rush wouldn't be an issue. When we got inside, Drew, Abby, Grace, and Maddie were all waiting for us with popcorn, candy, and pop. I looked at surprisingly at Gavin.

"The gang is back," he smiled. All I could think of was, is there anything this guy can't or wouldn't do for me. I wasn't able to come up with anything which meant I was with the most amazing guy in the world.

After the movie, we went to the local bakery for some hot chocolate. The warmth felt great after walking there in the icy cold air.

"Ok, I don't want to ruin a night but making everything awkward, but Laura, we all owe you an apology. You were right, we've been so worried to spend time with you. We didn't know what to say or how we'd react if you were sad. We were dumb to shut you out at the time you really needed is the most. We're sorry. Can you forgive us?" I smiled. Maybe things would start to become more normal after all.

A week later I went to the movies again but this time with Rosie. She was quieter without her mom but I could tell she was excited about the movie. Her mom had been so sweet and when she dropped her off, gave Rosie enough money for my ticket and snacks too. We sat in the quiet theater waiting for the ads to start. Rosie talked some about school but then asked all of a sudden if my dad lived with me or if he moved like her dad did. I told her my dad lives with me but that I have friends who have dad's who live elsewhere, so she's not alone. She smiled. The ads started and the lights began to dim. We sat back and enjoyed the movie. I felt that the more I began to know Rosie, the more we began to feel like true friends versus a pair set up through a volunteer group. As much as I had thought I'd like a little sister, I have to admit that having someone to do these types of "sister dates" with again felt great and was just what I needed most.

CHAPTER THIRTEEN

Journal entry:

Today Laura and I had a sister date. We got milkshakes and went for a walk at Bradley Park. Sometimes I'm still amazed by how fast time has gone. I still remember when we were little girls playing dress up and school, and when we'd sit back and dream about days like this. Days where we'd be able to go do our own thing and be old enough to drive. Well, at least I'm to that point. Haha. Poor Laura's not quite there. Today we talked about more dreams, bigger dreams. College, marriage, even kids. Laura said she's thinking about researching cellular neuroscience in college and something about myelination in neurons with multiple sclerosis. She's such a nerd but I love her. She also talked about Drew, who she's liked for a long time. I don't know what she sees in that guy. He's nice but just not the guy for her. I'm always mentioning how great Gavin is, but she never seems to think of him as more than a friend which I don't understand. Gavin is so good to her and so polite and respectful. He's the type of guy I'd trust to take care of my little sister, but not Drew. Hopefully, she'll figure that out on her own.

CHAPTER FOURTEEN

The rest of the spring semester came and went, remaining fairly uneventful. Gavin tried out to run for the track team and made it, so I often went to his races. A few races Rosie came with me to cheer him on. We had become pretty close over time and I really liked forward to our time together. We tried to get together at least twice a month for a movie, dinner, ice cream, or shopping. Pretty much all the fun girly things I used to do with Claire. Although I loved my time with Rosie, I was also glad to check off another goal from Claire's list: befriend an unlikely friend. In addition to Rosie, Nora's letters were coming with increased frequency, so I almost felt that I had met this goal twice. I received her latest letter last week:

Laura,

I hope you're doing well. Do you still miss Claire? I still miss Charlie, but I'm hoping if you don't miss Claire that maybe I'll be done being sad soon. School is going ok for me but my best friend, Crissy, is still not playing with me much. I wonder if it's because I cry a lot or if she misses Charlie too. Are you going to camp this year? My mom wants me to go because she says I need to have something fun to look forward to but I don't know if I want to go. My dad said I don't have to go if I don't want to.

Nora

Gavin came over on Saturday carrying his laptop. "Hey, let's go to the coffee shop for smoothies. I have something to show you."

We walked hand in hand to the shop, which was something we rarely do but for some reason, we did and it felt nice. Gavin pulled up a screen and played a video. The video showcased a girl, probably in her early twenties, discussing the importance of languages in her life. She claimed that knowing a few simple words in multiple languages allowed her to easily make friends anywhere she went. I was skeptical that she only knew a few simple words, but regardless, I kept watching intently.

"Our first word is hello. I am going to say it in eight common languages." She proceeded to say hello in Spanish, Chinese, French, Italian, Arabic, Japanese, German, and Portuguese. I was able to easily pronounce some of the languages but really struggled with a couple. Language classes have never been my forte, not even English, hence my interest in science. Gavin soon had hello, goodbye, help, and thank you memorized in all of the languages, while I was still mastering the difference between Hola and Hallo.

I laughed, "Perhaps this is one goal that was meant for Claire, not me." I kept practicing but found I wasn't super determined. "I'll get it someday. In other news, what are you thinking about for camp? I think I want to go back this summer but I'm worried it won't be as amazing as last summer. What do you think?"

Gavin smiled, "I already filled out my application. I definitely want to go back."

That night, I filled out my application for Towering Pines and became excited about the kids I would meet and the staff I'd befriend.

Before I knew it, sophomore year was over and it was time for camp training to start. Although I knew they'd still miss me, my leaving was an easier transition for my parents which meant I felt more at ease with leaving.

When Gavin and I arrived at camp, we were greeted by multiple staff including a few we knew from last year. "Hi, Madison!" I ran and gave her a hug.

"I'm so glad you're back Laura. I had us paired as a junior and senior counselor again this summer because last summer we worked so well together."

"That's great! I can't wait," I said enthusiastically.

I gave hugs to other staff too. Even though I didn't keep in great contact with them during the year, I still felt so deeply connected to them in a way I've never felt with my friends from home.

That night we sat around the campfire and got to know each other. Returning staff discussed favorite memories from last summer and new staff sat back and took it all in. It all felt perfect and I knew this was where I was truly supposed to be.

Our two weeks of training flew by and before I knew it, I was getting ready for our first group of girls. Madison and I played our "name that girl" game and before I knew it, I could match a name to a face for all seven of our girls: Jenna, Ruby, Chelsea, Vivian, Courtney, Evelyn, and Tasha. As we laid in our bunks quizzing each other, our camp director, Marsha, came in the cabin.

"Just wanted to let you girls know that another camper will be coming. You guys had her last year and we decided to place her with you again because she's had a rough year with her brother passing away."

I felt a sigh of relief knowing I'd be seeing her soon, "It's Nora." Marsha looked surprised until I added that I keep in contact with Nora throughout the year and knew that Charlie had passed away shortly before camp last year.

"I know this year has been very difficult for her, but we're going to make this week super memorable for her."

Sunday came and the girls arrived one by one. Although I was excited to meet all of them, I was anxiously awaiting Nora. While I was helping Evelyn unpack, I heard the cabin door open to reveal Nora. She had grown several inches and looked substantially skinnier than last summer. You could see some bones through her slender frame. Her eyes had dark circles, revealing the trauma this girl had undergone since Charlie was first diagnosed. She saw me and immediately ran to give me a hug. Unexpectedly, she started to cry.

"I'm so glad to see you, Laura." I felt the same way.

The week was really hard for me because I felt I needed to spend as much time with Nora as possible without neglecting the other girls in the cabin. Sensing my concern, the camp director actually added another counselor to our cabin.

"Laura, I can tell you have a special connection with Nora. According to her parents, this past year has been overwhelming for her, so we really want you to focus your time to help her in any way you can."

I was awoken from little sniffles and cries a few bunks from me. I knew it was Nora. I put on my warmer sweatshirt and went over to her.

"Hey Nora, let's go outside." She slowly got up and put on her sweatshirt and shoes.

We walked about a hundred yards to the waterfront and sat on a bench in the sand. The air was cool but the rhythmic splashing of the waves felt calming. Before I could say a word, Nora hugged me and cried as I've never seen anyone cry before. It reminded me of when I used to cry after Claire died. Long, exhausting tears. I held her tight and stroked her hair. Losing a sibling was so hard but I'm fortunate that I was a little older. I imagine that at ten, all you feel is confused and alone.

Nora cried for what felt like hours and when she calmed, we talked for what seemed like even more hours. Nora talked about a multitude of emotions including missing Charlie, abandonment be friends, seeing her parents cry all the time, and one I hadn't thought of, fear that she too would get cancer.

"My mom said his kind was genetic. She blames herself that she might have given it to him. All I can think of is that I don't want it. If my twin had it, I could too." Then she looked at me with deep sad eyes and said, "Laura, what do you think death is like?"

I've thought about this very question a million times but still didn't have an answer. "I imagine it's as peaceful as the waves and that you don't know what's happening, but you feel calm. I don't know what you believe, but I believe in God and that people go to Heaven. We can't even imagine how perfect Heaven is, but I think that when you go there, everyone you once loved is there to welcome you and even those you never met, like great -great grandparents. I imagine beautiful waterfalls and gorgeous sunsets. No one is ever sad in Heaven and everything is perfect. I think you get to do the things you loved doing. Like Claire, she loved softball, so I imagine her playing softball. And you know what, I've talked to Claire about Charlie and told her to watch out for him like a big sister, so I'm sure he's playing softball too."

Nora smiled, "After he was diagnosed, he was too weak to run and play. I hope he's able to run and play in Heaven."

I told her that no one in Heaven is sick and no one has cancer. "Charlie can run and play and laugh. Unfortunately, we still miss them and even though we know they're OK, part of us feels lost, but I know we'll see them again. It's ok to be sad, and it's OK to cry, but we have to keep living. We need to enjoy the time we have here because we only have one life." I gave Nora another hug. We sat there until the sun came up. That night was one I'll never forget.

The rest of that week seemed to turn around for Nora. She started to smile and tried to make friends. I still occasionally caught times where she was tearing up, but she would quickly wipe her tears away and keep playing.

The night before the girls left, Nora asked if I'd go for a walk with her. We walked on the trail to a small clearing in the woods. We laid on our backs and looked up at the stars.

"Laura, I'm scared to go back home. What if I get really sad again? I don't have friends at home anymore and all of Charlie's stuff is still at home which makes it harder. I wish I could just stay here."

"I know what you mean. I always struggle going home too because camp is an escape from reality. At home, I'm always known as the girl whose sister died but at camp, I'm just another girl. But you know what, home can be really great too because home is where you remember the good memories. For example, there's a big stain on our downstairs couch cushion from when I made Claire laugh so hard that juice flew out her nose. We tried so hard to clean it but couldn't get it out so we turned the cushion over. I don't think my mom has ever seen it, but whenever I miss Claire, instead of thinking of something sad, I go look at the stain on the couch. I know it's silly but it helps me. Do you have anything like that?"

Nora laughed. "When we were five, Charlie and I drew on his closest wall with permanent markers. We started to draw a dog and cat but Mom found us halfway through, so we had a dog without legs and a cat without a head. She couldn't get it off the wall and claimed she would just paint over it but she never has. I had forgotten about that." Nora laughed a little. "It seems like there are more bad memories than good though. Did I ever tell you that Charlie died at home? He died in his bed and my mom, dad, and I all sat there with him. That's why I hate being at home. To me, it's not home, it's where Charlie died."

All of a sudden, I started to cry. I can't imagine what Nora is experiencing. Claire died unexpectedly and suddenly. Nora knew Charlie was dying and actually sat with him as he took his last breath. She's so young and has already gone through more than most adults I know. I held her tight and we cried together.

The next morning I helped Nora pack her bag. We were both quiet and I honestly felt like I could cry at any moment. Amazingly, I held it together. I had encouraged Nora to ask her mom and dad if she could go see a grief counselor that specifically works with children who have lost loved ones. She said she would and promised to keep in touch with me.

Shortly after packing, her parents arrived. As her dad grabbed her bags, her mom pulled me aside.

"Laura, you are truly a blessing to our family. I barely know you, but I know that you are so important to Nora and have helped her immensely. I know that this week was probably very difficult for her, but I felt more at ease when I knew you were back this summer. Nora confides in you. She trusts you and tells me that you understand because you lost your sister. I'm so sorry you've had to go through something so tragic too. How are you doing?"

"Camp is my escape, so today I'm doing OK. When summer ends and I return to reality, I may feel differently. Nora is a great kid and I was so happy when I found out she was coming back this summer. We had a good week. Lots of hugs and tears, but overall a good week."

Her mom started to cry. " I just want her to be happy again. I want her to reconnect with her friends and get back to doing the things she loved, but she just doesn't have that spark about her anymore. I just don't know what to do."

I told her mom that I suggested a grief counselor and that Nora was open to trying. "You really are a miracle worker! We've been trying for a year to get Nora to agree to see someone and she always refuses. I do think it might help to have someone to talk to."

"She can also keep writing me. I'm always here."

She hugged me and thanked me for everything. Then she left to meet Nora at the car.

Gavin knew that saying goodbye to Nora was going to be difficult for me, so he planned a date night once we drove back home. Now that I'm tan and looking more fit from running during camp games all day long, I decided to wear a cute knee-length sundress with wedges. Gavin came over at six to pick me up and we headed for Big Al's because I was craving some delicious pancakes. Gavin always thought breakfast for dinner sounded awful, but I love it and luckily he's willing to put up with it occasionally.

I ordered my short stack with strawberry sauce while Gavin picked french toast. We chatted about our week. His week was a little more low key than mine. No near drownings. The only thing he had to worry about were the ten girls who vied for his attention.

"It's just funny. I'm just an average guy. I don't know why all these little girls get crushes on me."

I smiled, "Pretty sure I know why."

After our breakfast for dinner, we went to the movies and then headed home. "Gavin, Nora asked me something this week and I've been curious to learn your thoughts. What do you think death is like?"

He sat and pondered for what seemed like forever. "I guess I haven't really thought about it. I don't know."

As much as I love Gavin, it's moments like this when I realize that our lives are so different. The pain and the heartache with losing Claire is at the very core of my being. I've thought about death a million times and Gavin hasn't had to ever think about it.

He's a lucky guy.

The rest of the summer passed quickly. Campers came and went. Memories were made and I loved every second of it. Nora sent me a couple letters and she mentioned that she was seeing a counselor and had joined a sibling support group.

"They understand. They aren't afraid when I cry. I finally belong somewhere again." I was so happy for Nora and I totally understood how she felt. Unfortunately, I was leaving my place where I belonged and was returning back to school, where I still felt like an outsider.

CHAPTER FIFTEEN

My seventeenth birthday came and went and soon it was the beginning of junior year. I had high hopes for this year including continuing to be Rosie's big sister, doing well in school, and if all goes well, going on the church mission trip to Nicaragua during spring break. I hadn't mentioned the latter to my parents yet, but the registration deadline was quickly approaching.

One night at dinner I mentioned the upcoming trip and my interest in going. "That sounds like fun. We should definitely sign you up. Where are they going?"

I swallowed hard. I had left out the small detail that the trip was in a third world country. I coughed slightly as I answered.

"Ooh, I hope you're not getting sick. Now, where is the trip? It sounded like you said Nicaragua but you must have said Nevada."

"Actually, your first thought is correct. It's in Nicaragua. We'll be teaching English in schools, helping to build a church, going to an orphanage, and leading church services in the evening. The trip is just over a week long and it sounds like an amazing opportunity."

My parents looked at each other slightly, as if to discuss their thoughts. Sometimes it seems like they can read each other's thoughts or that they somehow communicate with their eyes.

"Your Mom and I thought about it and we think it would be OK based on a few conditions. First, we want to see who the chaperones are and if we don't know them well, one of us would like to go to make sure you're safe. And second, we're sure the trip will be expensive, so we'd like you to do a few more chores around the house to help earn your way."

"Both sound fine to me! Thanks, guys."

"Is Gavin going too?" they asked.

I explained that we had talked about it but he wasn't sure if he'd be able to. "It might be good for me to step out of my comfort zone and try something new and meet some new people."

The registration deadline came and I was all signed up. A couple parents my mom knew were going so they decided it would be OK for me to go without them. Gavin decided not to go meaning I'd be going on this adventure alone. Our church is fairly large and the trip is open to kids in other area churches so there was a good chance I wouldn't know anyone very well.

One Sunday after church, all the kids and parents met to discuss the trip details and to have a meet and greet. There were a few kids I recognized but no one I knew personally. During the meeting, we played ice breaker games, discussed what to expect, and learned some key Spanish words, like hi, bye, my name is, and how are you. The group leaders discussed things that we may find hard, especially the level of poverty.

At one point, we broke into pairs for more get to know you activities. The girl I was paired with was tall and slender with short brown hair. Her name tag said "Audrey." Together we talked for about ten minutes. Audrey lived in a neighboring town so I had never met her before. She was a junior like myself and hoped to be an engineer someday. I was excited to be talking to another science nerd which is a rare find for a teenage girl. Before we knew it, time was up. We didn't have time to discuss much, but I could tell she'd become one of my closest friends on the trip.

The day ended with final details and group prayer. I've always believed in God but Claire dying has weakened my faith. Claire was always the very faithful, God loving type. I hoped that this trip would reconnect me to God and His greater purpose.

Spring break soon arrived and my bags were packed for Nicaragua. I was nervously excited to start my journey. My parents dropped me off at church to ride the bus to the airport, and of course, my mom teared up and all she could mumble was, "please be safe."

"I'll never leave the group. I'll be safe," I promised.

I loaded my stuff and hopped on the bus. There was an open seat next to Audrey, the girl I met at the meet and greet. I soon discovered a lot about her. In addition to loving science, she also loves gymnastics. She talked about her family, including three brothers and a sister. Then came the dreaded, how many siblings do you have question. I still struggle with answering because, in my mind, I still have one sister. Claire will always be my sister, even when she's gone.

"Just one, an older sister." I prayed she wouldn't ask for more details about Claire and my prayer was answered.

Soon we were on the plane and continuing to talk. We discussed different science topics as two nerds would. Then she asked if I had a boyfriend, so I gushed about Gavin and then asked her about any special guys.

"I don't have a boyfriend, but the guy I like is actually on this trip. Greg, do you know him?" I didn't but was definitely going to figure out who he was.

Once we landed in Managua, we gathered our bags and sent through customs. My new passport finally had a stamp which was incredibly exciting to a small town girl.

We soon arrived at our first stop, an orphanage on the outskirts of Managua. The orphanage housed approximately seventy-five children who lived in small bunkhouses holding about ten kids based on age and gender. While we were there, the boys would be tent camping and the girls would stay in available bunks. My bed was in the younger girls bunkhouse that had about eight girls aged three to six. I almost cried when I realized that this was all they had, a bed with old tattered bedding and clothes that had been donated from America that say "Superbowl Champs" but boasted the name of the opponent that year, not the actual champion. Despite how little they had, the girls were thriving and happy. They all hugged me as I entered and helped me carry my bag to my bed.

That night, all the children put on a song and dance show for us. They wore brightly colored costumes and played a variety of tropical sounding instruments. A few courageous members of our group, including Audrey, even got up to dance with the kids. Together we all clapped, laughed, and enjoyed our time together. I was again amazed by the fact that these children have so little and yet seem so happy and content. That's a feeling I hoped to have someday.

The next day we split up into groups with some of us teaching English in classes, others helping with general repair and maintenance of buildings, and others helping with the nursery children. My group started with general maintenance. We were to collect all the rocks we could, which would be crushed to create a foundation for a new bunkhouse. Soon after starting I became sore. My hands bled from a sharp rock and my back hurt from bending. I wanted to keep in good spirits but gosh, this was my spring break. Soon Greg offered me his gloves which I gladly accepted. "My hands are all calloused anyways from playing guitar, so I really don't need them." I kindly thanked him and made a mental note to tell Audrey. It was clear why she liked him.

We worked diligently for two hours and then we switched to the school group. Although we were all tired and covered in dirt, the children were excited to see us. They showed us their small one-room school, rickety playground, and open stalled outhouse right next to the slide. I guess privacy isn't a necessity after all. We worked in the classroom for two hours, assisting with an art project, teaching a few English words, and helping with math. Luckily I could count to twenty in Spanish. Following a lunch of rice and beans, my group helped in the nursery. The orphanage housed ten children under the age of two, most of whom were in the process of being adopted. Although I loved my time playing and cuddling with the younger ones, I felt so sad knowing that the older children would probably never be adopted. Everyone always wants to adopt a baby, one baby. I vowed to myself to one day adopt an older child, maybe birth siblings.

That night after dinner and church, Audrey and I sat out under the stars. The sound of monkeys could be heard in the distance.

"I just can't believe I'm here. It's so beautiful." I told Audrey that I felt the same way and yet, I felt alone. It was nice to not be known as the girl who lost a sister and yet, being around people who know gives you a support system. I missed my parents and I really missed Gavin. I hadn't realized how big of a part of my life he was.

Like clockwork, Audrey said, "So, tell me about this boyfriend. How did you meet? What's he like?"

I told Audrey all about Gavin, the boy next door. "I've known him forever, but we've only dated for a couple of years. He's a great guy. Very kind, very giving. I'm very blessed."

I told her about Gregory offering me his work gloves. She was jealous she wasn't in his work group. We sat there and talked for a few hours. "It's weird. I've known you for only a couple of days and yet I know we're going to be best friends."

Although it was sad to leave the orphanage, I looked forward to our next stop, a small village on the shore of the Pacific ocean, about two hours away. Our bus kicked up large clouds of dirt as we maneuvered the small windy roads. I was amazed at the small homes I saw. One, maybe two roomed shacks with makeshift out-houses and wild chickens and pigs running amuck.

We finally made it to the small village and were happily greeted by ten neighborhood school children, all except one wearing a school uniform. The children ranged in age from about five to twelve and were talking so fast in Spanish that I couldn't catch what they were saying. My group leader trans-lated, "They're very happy you're all here and they want to play baseball."

Baseball was always more of a Claire thing. I've never been ath-letic and I didn't even have a mitt with me. Looking around, I no-ticed that all the children had was a piece of wood they used for a bat and a ball. No mitts, no real bat.

We started to play and used rocks or bushes as our bases. The longer we played, the more fun we had. It was my turn to bat. Rob-erto, one of the older boys, pitched the ball and I made contact. The ball speeded quickly and hit Roberto straight in the head. He fell over but being the tough boy he was, he didn't cry. His head swelled within seconds. While all of the Americans surrounded him with concern, his dad came out and simply patted his back and said he was fine. It was then I realized that even if something was wrong, there's no hospital and no money to even go to the hospital. These kids have to tough it out.

The next day, Audrey and I walked on the dusty road in our small neighborhood. Towards the east was the small town which housed a church and a fishing area and towards the west was where the area school was located. We walked east. On our walk, we spotted one of the boys we had met the day before, the boy without the school uniform. He was at the fishing area with an older boy, perhaps his brother. The rest of the town was bare of children who were all at school. Audrey and I were curious why this boy wasn't in school too. As we continued to walk, the two boys saw us and waved us over. The younger boy started cheerily taking in Spanish. Sensing our confusion, the older boy laughed and started talking in English.

"We're so glad your group is here to work with us. I'm Jorge and this is my brother Juan Jose. Our dad is the Pastor, Pedro." We chatted for some time when Audrey finally decided to ask why Juan Jose wasn't in school. Jorge frowned and we sensed his hesitation. "I'm so sorry for asking. I can see you're uncomfortable. We don't need to talk about it."

"Oh no, it's ok. It's just very hard for me to discuss. I feel very sad about the situation. You see, our family is very poor. In addition to Juan Jose and myself, were have three sisters and one brother. I'm the oldest and as the oldest, it is my responsibility to financially provide for our family. My parents have spent their whole life paying for and supporting my education so that I can get a good paying job, but that is at the cost of my siblings future. In order for me to to be educated, my parents can't afford to send the others to any schooling, even primary. Next year, I'll move to Managua to attend university and after I graduate and get a good job, I hope I can pay for all my siblings to attend school, even though by then, most will be past graduation age. Sadly, this is the reality for a lot of families. We can't afford to educate all the children, so oftentimes, parents will select one child, ideally, the oldest or child deemed to have the greatest potential, and will invest all resources into ensuring that child succeeds. I wish we had a system like America where every child is educated, but that isn't a reality here."

I couldn't believe what I was hearing. Imagine only being able to educate one child and pray that they are successful and can help support the family.

"Wow, I had no idea."

"No worries, most people don't but here it's normal." I decided at that moment that I didn't want it to be the normal, at least not for this family.

"How much does it cost a family to send one child to school?"

Jorge replied, "The cost of school itself is not too expensive, just uniforms, books, and supplies, but what is expensive is the lost income and productivity of having a child spend time at school. If Juan Jose was at school, our family would not have someone tending to the garden and chickens which not only is important to feed the family, but we sell extras to the locals. This means we'd have less food and financial resources. Not that I don't think we could figure it out, but it would make our livelihood more unpredictable."

We continued to talk to them for more time and I grew to really enjoy them. They invited Audrey and me over for lunch. "We were just on a short walk. We don't know our group's schedule. We'd love to come but can we first check with our leader."

"Oh yes, of course. Thanks for talking with us." Juan Jose smiled and gave us both a hug goodbye. It broke my heart to know his day, and probably the rest of his life, was spent gardening, fishing, and taking care of chickens.

When we got back to our group, we discovered that our group would be volunteering at the church with Pedro and were told the whole church group would be spending lunch with Jorge and Juan Jose's family. We walked to the church which definitely didn't resemble any American church. The building was one room made up of a stone wall with large openings where a traditional window would fit. The ceiling was nonexistent, but a large palm grew over the building and provided the necessary shade. Pews and the pulpit were made from rocks mortared together. Altogether, I'd say the small church could hold up to twenty churchgoers unless they were ok with standing. Pedro and two children entered, presumably Juan Jose's sisters. Pedro introduced himself and his family in Spanish. I caught the children's names to be Maria, who was about six and Veronica, who was a little older than Juan Jose. He talked about the church while one of our leaders translated. "Our church is a blessing and gift from God above. We have been working as a community to build this church for a few years now and we finally have the main structure completed. Our goal for today is general cleaning inside and starting the roof. We have other locals coming to help. Be safe, have fun, and thank you."

Audrey and I worked on general cleaning and left the roof to those who knew more about construction. Being that the small room had been without a roof for so long, the inside was full of dirt, leaves, and animal droppings. Before knew it, it was lunch. I spent my lunch talking some more with Jorge and his younger brother Miguel Santiago who was fifteen. I discovered that Miguel is a local fishermen expert. His days are spent in the ocean on his small fishing rig each day and catches fish for his family and sells out trades fish for other goods to other locals.

"So really, you all work hard to support your family."

Jorge smiled, "Yes, God and family come above all."

I discovered that Gabriela, who's thirteen, and Veronica help their mom sew and cook. They sell their goods in the community and once a week, they take the bus to a larger neighboring community to sell at the market. Even little Maria helps with cleaning and assisting Juan Jose in the garden.

I felt I was overstepping my boundaries and asking too personal questions, but being that we're leaving tomorrow, I had to know. "How much money would your family need to make sure that all of you could go to school."

Jorge stopped and thought about it. "After I graduate, I hope to give my family at least one thousand Cordoba each month which is equivalent to about thirty United States dollars. Right now they live on about one thousand Cordoba a month, so that should be enough to make up for any lost income from my siblings attending school. Of course, it depends on the job I am able to get. I'd love to provide more if I can."

"So, thirty dollars a month is all that stands in the way of your siblings attending school?"

"Yes, give or take a dollar or so."

"Can I just give you that money or hold a fundraiser for your family?"

"That would be a huge blessing but is not necessary. I'll be able to provide once I graduate but that will take some time."

"Jorge, I don't mean to sound like a spoiled rich girl, especially because I wouldn't call my family rich for American standards, but thirty-four dollars is nothing to most Americans. It's the decision between a new shirt or not. Please, let me help your family. It would mean the world to me."

Jorge started crying and yelled to his father in Spanish. Pastor Pedro came running to Jorge with tears rolling down his face. Jorge pointed to me as he talked with his father. He later translated his father's words as, "He is saying that your group is a blessing and he wants to say thank you for your generosity."

"Tell him I'll talk to the group and before we leave, we will leave some starter money with you and that I'll keep sending more every month. You can always rely on me sending the money. I promise."

Later that night I discussed the situation with my group. "If you are willing, I'd appreciate any amount. This family and area families are living on one dollar a day. Please consider. I plan on giving Pastor Pedro the money tomorrow."

One by one, each group member walked up to me and gave me varying amounts of money. Once all fifteen people had given,

I counted the money and we had collected two hundred and fifty dollars. "Thanks, everyone. This money will really make a difference. Pastor Pedro plans on sending the children to school and giving money to other locals who need assistance also."

The next day, Audrey, one of the leaders, and I walked to the church. Pastor Pedro was there with Juan Jose, who ran out to greet us with a hug. I handed him the money. "Para su familia."

He opened the envelope and saw the money. "Muchos gracias." Then Juan Jose put up his hand to signal wait and ran off quickly. He soon returned with a mango and a picture. He rattled off something in Spanish and our group leader translated, "This mango is for you as a thank you. Also, I drew this picture of my family. Don't forget us. We'll never forget you. God bless." Then he hugged us all.

"I won't forget you, ever. I hope to see you again someday."

The plane ride home was bittersweet. I was glad to go home and see my parents and Gavin, but I truly loved the people of Nicaragua and felt truly blessed by them. I'll never forget my trip. The orphans I worked with and the locals like Juan Jose and his family. I'm beginning to see that even though my life get purposeless for so long, that I do have the power to do something, to make a difference. And I will.

That night when I told Gavin all about my experience, I got a little too excited and relayed my plan for us to adopt a child from Nicaragua after we get married. He looked at me kind of dumbfounded and shocked.

"Umm, just ignore that. Too much heat and I'm not thinking." I paused and finally said, "Well, I'm tired and should get going."

As I got up to leave, he grabbed my hand and said, "Adopting a child sounds perfect. Sleep well."

Returning to school after such an incredible experience was

really hard. Abby talked about her family's vacation to Florida and laying on the beach. Maddie and Grace talked about going shopping and getting their nails done. When it was my turn, I said that Nicaragua was amazing but exhausting from all the work. The girls looked surprised.

"Work? You actually worked," they asked in unison.

I talked about helping build a bunkhouse at the orphanage and cleaning and roofing the church. Grace said it sounded "awful." Luckily, I had made plans to meet up with Audrey, Greg, and a few others from the trip during the upcoming weekend. I knew Gavin would love them and feel like he has more in common with them also.

The weekend came quickly and before we knew it, Gavin and I were out bowling with my new friends. We all laughed and had a great time discussing our trip and everyone getting to know Gavin.

"So Gavin, why didn't you come?" they all asked.

"Laura and I do so much together. I wanted this to be her thing, and it honestly seems like it was good for her. Really helped her deal with her pain in losing Claire."

My face started to flush. I hadn't told anyone about Claire. Audrey paused, "Um, can I ask who's Claire?" Gavin looked questionably at me.

"Gavin, I didn't tell anyone. It was so nice not being around people who knew. No one to feel sorry for me. I felt normal." I looked around at my small group of new friends, "I know you're all confused, but Claire was, is, my sister. She died just over two years ago in a car accident. She was killed by a drunk driver. It's been really hard for me and I just didn't want to have to talk about it on the trip, a trip where part of my intent was to just get away from all of that. It's not that I don't think I'd you guys as friends. I didn't hide it because of that, I just didn't want to think about it."

They all smiled, "We understand. Want to keep bowling?" I couldn't help but smile because for once, I wasn't being treated as breakable.

CHAPTER SIXTEEN

Journal entry:

I almost hate writing this in my journal. Seems so morbid and crazy, but I actually a dream last night that I died. It felt so real that it almost makes me scared. I'm sure it was just a crazy dream but it is making me think about what's really important in life. Sometimes I get so focused on things that don't matter, like trying to ace every test and be uber-athletic. While they are important, they aren't what should drive and define me. When I really think about it, if I died, I'd want to be remembered by my faith and how I loved others. I know some people don't believe in God, but I honestly can't believe that God couldn't exist. How is it possible for nature to be so in sync and work as if in unison? How is it possible for a human to miraculously form from cells? I recognize that there is pain and heartache and that I've been spared from the worst of it, but I honestly don't feel like God gives us pain... The work of evil does and God works with us and through others to get us through it.

Other than faith, my family and friends are the most important thing to me. I haven't always been the best at showing my family and friends how much they mean to me. If something were to happen, I hope they know that they make my life worth living. They make me happy.

I just can't get over how real it felt. Eerily real.

I sobbed as I closed the journal. Claire wrote this entry less than a month before she died.

CHAPTER SEVENTEEN

My senior year had finally arrived. The year every teen looks forward to because it marks the beginning of the rest of your life. I had college tours to take and applications with essays to write. I had senior pictures to take and prom to look forward to. I must admit that after all the stuff I've been through, all the biggies of the senior year didn't seem that exciting, especially after looking over college applications. Why is it that every single school from coast to coast wants you to write about a time you overcame adversity? This might be the only time that having a dead sister turns out to be useful, but honestly, I'd rather be one of those kids who have such a privileged life that you have to make a hangnail sound like the biggest crisis to face the northern hemisphere since the cold war.

My parents and I went with Gavin and his parents on a few tours over the summer. Although we hadn't narrowed it down to our top choices, we had officially agreed to go to the same school. Although my parents love Gavin, I sensed their hesitation with that decision. I heard countless "don't limit yourself," "what if you break up," and "you can always visit each other." But when it came down to it, being at the same school as Gavin was the only thing I was certain that I wanted and he felt the same.

I also knew I wanted to be close to home, mainly so that I have the option to come home on weekends. Honestly, there were still times where I feel very down and just need the support of my parents. I knew they felt the same way, so it was best for everyone's mental well-being for me to be within a couple hours of home.

As the school year progressed, I narrowed my search and my top contender was Kelner University, a small school close to home which offered a great science program.

I sat down that night and started my application and essay for Kelner University. The essay topic, of course, was to discuss the greatest obstacle you've ever had to overcome. I put my hands on the keyboard and started typing away...

As I sat at my computer thinking about what I've overcome, I honestly wished nothing would have come to mind. I wished I struggled to think of anything or could somehow make something sound like more adversity than what it really is, but I can't.

When I was fifteen, my older sister, Claire, was killed by a drunk driver. Claire was an all- American, down to earth, the girl next door kind of girl. Everyone loved her and was truly devastated by her death. The difference is that everyone else, other than my immediate family, moved on. Everyone else continued to do well in school, attend parties and dances, and overall just fit in, except me. I struggled to find enjoyment in learning and my best friends now found me breakable and unrelatable, so they moved on without me. The only thing that gave me solace in my grief was an old tattered book I found in Claire's room, her journal. Typical teenage girls would write only of boys, shopping, and friends but Claire wrote of her hopes, dreams, and goals. She had a bucket list and I made it my mission to accomplish her dreams for her. I've spent multiple summers volunteering at a camp, an experience which gave me hope in what felt like a hopeless world. I've befriended individuals I never would have dreamed of befriending. I've gone on a mission trip to Central America and was truly changed by the lifestyle and their live life to the fullest and a thankful attitude. I've explored new hobbies and attempted to learn new languages. I still have larger goals to attain, including getting married, saving someone's life, and writing a book. Through my experiences, I've discovered more about Claire than I could've imagined. I learned of her enjoyment for trying new things and her kind heart for helping all kinds of people. My experiences have also allowed me to focus on something other than my grief and given me the opportunity to do things I never would have sought out on my own.

I can't say that I've fully overcome my grief, but each day I get stronger. Each day I learn more about how to use my experience for good and develop a purpose for my past, present, and future.

I sat back and reread my essay. I had so much more details I could add, but I needed to stay in the word count. It was a great rough draft and maybe, just maybe, whoever reads it will decide to admit me to Kelner University.

I stood at the mailbox and slowly turned the letter as I felt the thickness. Too thick for a rejection I hoped. I slowly walked to Gavin's and checked his box. He had a letter too. He must have seen me because he ran out. "Laura, are they here?" I handed him his and we both immediately opened them. Accepted. We were both accepted. My letter contained another document. I began reading aloud.

"Dear Ms. Russell, we are pleased to inform you that you have been selected as the freshman class nominee for the "Above the Obstacles" award, which is given to a student who was able to overcome difficult life circumstances and continue to persevere in academics. Please accept our condolences for your sister's death. On behalf of the Kelner University faculty, I am pleased to offer you a scholarship for your first year's tuition. This scholarship is renewed annually for students who continue to receive top honors in their classes. Congratulations and we look forward to having you join us in the class of 2016."

I was dumbfounded and Gavin was ecstatic! I didn't even realize this scholarship program existed and I assumed there must be someone who has had a more tragic life than I have. Don't get me wrong, Claire dying had been horrible and heartbreaking but I knew there are others who were worse off than me. Despite that, I would gladly accept my scholarship.

Mom and Dad were beyond excited. Finances have been a little tighter being that mom reduced her hours at the hospital since Claire died. That night we had Gavin's family over for an informal celebration.

The rest of senior year went by so fast. Gavin and I went to Prom together and had an amazing time, like we always did. A few weeks later, we walked across the stage as we collected our diplomas. Finally, high school was over and I was excited to begin the next stage.

A month before college started, I unexpectedly received a call from Nora. "So great to hear from you. I didn't even know you had my phone number. You must have found it online." She confirmed that she had. "I'm so glad you picked up. Laura, I really need your help."

Before I knew it, I was in my car and driving as fast as possible to a small town four hours away. My shaking fingers quickly dialed those three numbers no one ever wants to dial. "911, what's your emergency?"

"Hi, my name is Laura Russell. One of my friends named Nora Kingston just called me and said she's thinking of taking her life. I live four hours away and need police to her house immediately."

The dispatcher took Nora's information and then connected me to Nora's local police department.

"Hi, miss. The dispatcher informed me that you talked to your friend and she said she's thinking of taking her life. We are on our way to the house. Can you tell me the full conversation?"

"Nora is a thirteen-year-old girl I worked with at camp. Her twin brother died from cancer three years ago. She just called me and said she was so glad I answered because she was about to take her dad's prescription drugs and wanted to talk to me before she did. She said she just couldn't do it anymore and she missed Charlie too much. I told her I was on my way to her house and she promised me she wouldn't do anything, but I live four hours away."

"Miss, we are at the house. Do you know where the girl's parents might be?"

"I'm guessing work, but I don't know. If the door is locked, break out down. Just save her."

With that, I was on hold, a hold that felt like forever. Finally, the officer can't back on the line. "She's ok. You were right. She had the medicine in hand but didn't take any. You saved her life. I told her you're on your way. We will try to contact her parents."

I started crying, "Thank you so much!"

The drive felt like forever but I knew she was safe and that's all that mattered. I called my mom and explained. My mom sounded dumbfounded. "Oh my. Oh no. Poor thing. She's so lucky she had you to call. What if... I won't think that way. You be safe Laura. I don't want you driving back late. Dad and I are coming."

I finally arrived at Nora's house at seven that night. I rang the doorbell and her mom answered. She was crying.

"Oh, Laura. You're my miracle." She hugged me for a long time and then led me to the living room. Nora sat on the couch with her dad. When she saw me, she ran to hug me. "You actually came."

We all sat down and decompressed. "We've all been talking and we think it best for Nora stay at the Vivianna Center, a center for girls struggling with mental health concerns like depression, eating disorders, and suicidal intentions. They also have a lot of family counseling which will be good for all of us. The police officers got ahold of them and let us know that they do have a room for Nora, so we'll go tomorrow."

Her dad started crying, "Thank heavens we have a tomorrow."

"Can Laura and I talk alone?" Nora asked.

We went to Nora's room and sat in silence for over a couple minutes. "So, Nora, what happened?"

"I don't know. I felt at the end of my rope. I just couldn't handle it all anymore. Missing Charlie, having difficulties making friends, feeling disconnected from my parents, and struggling to focus in school. The support group did help for a while but then I started to feel really down that so many kids my age have died. I'm not interested in anything. I go to school and then come home and just sit on the couch and watch mindless TV shows. I'm never hungry anymore. I just don't care."

"If I hadn't picked up, what would've happened?"

"I've been thinking for some time of doing something but I've never had the courage. Today I told myself that I would do it because it couldn't hurt more than I already felt but then I felt like I needed to talk to you first. I don't know what I would've done if you didn't answer. Maybe wait for you to call back but maybe not. I'm glad you're here. I just want to be happy again. Sometimes I try to remember what true happiness felt like but I don't remember. I wonder what the Vivianne Center will be like. I wonder if it'll help me."

We talked for an hour until the sound of the doorbell interrupted our conversation.

"Laura, you're parents are here," I said my goodbyes to Nora and her parents. "I'll see you tomorrow. Always remember, I'm here for you and I'll always be here for you."

That night, Mom, Dad, and I stayed in a hotel and of course, my parents used the opportunity to have an in-depth conversation.

"Have you ever felt like hurting yourself?" my mom asked.

"No, no. You have to know that I'd never do anything like that. Ever. Yes, there are times I'm sad and feel disjointed but I've never considered hurting myself. If I ever felt that way, I'd ask for help. You guys have been through so much and I'd never on purpose put you through more pain."

I could tell my parents felt relieved by my answer and they never brought up the subject again.

The next day Nora went to the Vivianne Center and I prayed she'd get the services she needed. I helped her settle in while her parents completed and the paperwork.

"Seems like a really nice place. Nice windows to let in the sun and look, your window overlooks the garden. Such beautiful flowers."

"Laura, have you ever thought about, well, you know?"

"Right after Claire died, I was really depressed. Nothing made me happy and I felt so alone. I knew I didn't want my life to feel that way and at the time, I truly believed I'd never feel happy again. I never considered hurting myself, but I didn't really see the point in anything anymore. Now that I'm older, I can see that although there are moments I miss Claire, there are more moments that I'm happy and not missing her. I can see that I still have a future and things to look forward to like college, a career, marriage, buying a house, kids, and traveling. Losing Claire has changed my life but it doesn't have to end it. Same with you. Losing Charlie is awful, especially so young, but you still have a million things you will do in your life. You can look forward to all the good things to come, those things little girls dream of. They are hard to imagine now, but if you kill yourself, you'll never get the opportunity to experience those great things."

Nora started crying and said, "I just want to feel happy again."

As I hugged her, I reassured her, "I promise that you will. You are going to grow up, find a career that allows you to make a difference, fall in love, and have beautiful babies. Maybe your experience with losing Charlie will allow you to help others, just like how losing Claire has allowed me to understand what you're going through. You'll be OK, you just have to make it through this rough patch. Promise me you'll never hurt yourself no matter how sad and alone you feel."

Nora hesitated and then finally promised. A promise she always kept.

CHAPTER EIGHTEEN

"Laura Russell, Bachelor of Science in Education with a Minor in Biology." Upon hearing my name, I confidently walked across the stage to accept my college diploma. I had finally graduated from college and was ready to start my career. Gavin and I had already both secured jobs; I will be starting at an inner-city middle school as a science teacher and Gavin is set to start as an accountant at a well-known accounting firm.

After the ceremony, my parents and Gavin's greeted us with hugs and congratulations. I happened to see my mom wink at Gavin and upon seeing the wink, Gavin announced that he had planned a graduation getaway for us to celebrate prior to entering the real world.

"When?" I enthusiastically asked.

"Right now, our plane leaves in three hours. We better get going." My mom reassured me that she was in on the surprise and had already packed my bags.

"Gavin, where are we going?"

Gavin laughed, "Wouldn't you like to know."

We arrived at the airport and parked our car in the lot. We grabbed our bags and headed to check in at security. I still had no idea where we were going until Gavin handed me my ticket, Miami. Relaxing in the warm Florida air sounded amazing and Gavin must have sensed my excitement. "It's not what you think," was all he said.

We landed a few hours later and grabbed our rental car. Gavin started to drive for what felt like hours and it started to get dark. Soon we found out hotel, a cute inn in Key West. Gavin laughed "Here's our home for one night. Our big adventure starts tomorrow." As I lay in bed that night, I questioned what he could mean. Big adventure? Knowing Gavin, it could mean anything or nothing, maybe he's just being funny.

Beep, beep, beep. I rolled over to check the clock. You have to be kidding me, four a.m.! Three a.m. home time.

"Are you serious right now?"

Gavin smiled, "Come on, you need to take a shower and get packed up. We have to get going early enough so we can stop and get some rolls quick before departure."

"Departure?" I questioned.

"Yep, we need to be to the boat at six to load up our gear."

"A boat? What gear?"

Gavin explained that he had shipped all of our gear down a week ago. We were going island camping. I would be sleeping on a beach on a deserted island meaning I could cross off another of Claire's dreams.

The walk from our hotel to the port was quick but I tried to soak in some of the culture despite it being so dark. There were chickens running through the streets and as the sun began to rise, I noticed the brightly colored, almost tropical like, houses with cute front porches. It reminded me of my high school trip to Nicaragua but with more wealth. We were able to find a small peddler cart selling drinks and sweets. I had a strawberry smoothie and a cinnamon roll, both of which were delicious. We stopped in the ticketing area and were able to collect the two large bags that Gavin had shipped from home. The bags were filled with non-perishable food, two lightweight sleeping bags, dishes, and a small tent. We purchased jugs of water too being that the island had no running water.

The large boat slowly filled with an estimated two hundred passengers. I always try not to judge others, but most of these people did not look like the camping type. They were wearing nice clothes, makeup, and carrying expensive purses. Gavin explained that the boat carries campers and day-trippers. The day people would come back on the same boat tonight while the campers stay out on their own. I secretly hoped no one else is staying to camp.

We started talking to the couple sitting across from us, Dave and Catherine. They explained this was their first trip away from their two children, the oldest who was five and youngest three. Catherine explained how she always loved traveling and never realized it would be so emotional to leave their children for an adults only trip. I tried so hard to listen intently and really get to know the nice couple but all I could do was try to breathe deeply and not let the rocky boat get the best of me.

Gavin grabbed my hand, "Are you OK? You look very pale."

He flagged down one of the staff and secured a bag just in case I needed it. I prayed with all my might that I'd survive the ride. Although there were some others getting ill, I knew I would be so embarrassed if I too became one of them. I slowly sipped my ginger ale and closed my eyes. Soon Gavin was telling me that the island was in view and that I had made it.

We docked and gathered our camping supplies. We discovered that no one else would be camping and the only other people on the island were two park rangers and their families. We set up camp near the beach and I rejoiced in knowing we'd be able to hear the calming waves and quiet breeze as we slept at night. After setting up camp, we explored the island. The island housed an old fort used to protect the United States from intruders. The now abandoned fort had some areas of erosion but overall was in great condition; in fact, parts of the fort housed current rangers who would be our go to people in case of emergency. I was shocked to see that some of the ranger apartments actually had air conditioning units coming from a window so I imagined they had some form of generator. Our day was spent touring the fort, snorkeling in the water, and relaxing on the beach. The day trip guests left around three in the afternoon, meaning we had the beach to ourselves.

"Gavin, this is perfect. Thank you."

He put his arm around me and smiled, "We're staying two nights and I checked with one of the rangers and currently, no one else is slated to camp tomorrow night either." I couldn't believe it, two nights in this beautiful paradise.

We sat in silence staring at the sunset. Everything felt so perfect, so unbelievable. Sometimes I find myself thinking back to my life at fifteen. I was so scared and so lost. I never imagined that I'd ever feel happy again and yet, at this moment, I feel nothing but happiness.

"Gavin, what are you thinking about right now?"

He smiled, "Nothing too exciting. Just thinking about how much fun we had today. About how much fun we always have together."

All of a sudden a park ranger came up and interrupted our moment. "Hi, you two. I wanted to introduce myself and actually ask for some help. I'm Tim, one of the rangers here."

Gavin and I both introduced ourselves and explained where we are from and discussed how much we're enjoying the island.

"Well, I really hate to disrupt you both, but I could really use a strong set of arms to move something in the fort. Our other ranger, Chris, is sick and it's too heavy for my wife and kids. Gavin, would you be willing to help. I only need five minutes of your time."

"Not a problem," Gavin replied.

Both Gavin and I started to get up. "Laura, you can just wait here. Enjoy the sunset and I will be back as soon as I can."

I sat back down and continued to look at the beautiful ocean and think about my life. Graduation wasn't as emotional for me as I had feared, at least not like high school graduation. For high school, all I did was cry. Cry for myself, cry for Claire, and cry for my parents. I felt so sad that Claire couldn't be there for my big day and even sadder that Claire never had her graduation. It was scary for me that I was officially doing things she never got the opportunity to do and it seemed that going to college meant I was officially moving on with my life. I was leaving my childhood and my parents and trying to find my way. Graduating from college was different though. It felt exciting and empowering. I now have a degree and can start doing something I love, teaching science. I think Claire has been gone so long that the pain is slowly leaving and I'm starting to fully enjoy life again.

I could hear Gavin coming in the distance. I looked up and smiled. He was carrying something. It looked like food.

"Tim gave us some dessert for helping!" Gavin pulled out a gallon of ice cream.

"Gavin, how on earth are we ever going to eat that much ice cream?"

Gavin laughed as he handed me my spoon, "I don't know but if I remember correctly, you need to finish a whole gallon of ice cream with your future husband."

With that, Gavin was on one knee and opened a ring box containing the most beautiful ring I had ever seen. "Laura, I have loved you since we were little kids. I used to pray that one day you'd like me as more than just the boy next door and when we

Sally Joseph

began dating, I couldn't believe how lucky I was. Every day with you is great and every moment with you is an adventure. I can't go through another day without knowing if you will spend the rest of your life with me. Laura Russell, will you marry me?"

All I could do was smile as I managed to mumble the word, "Yes."

Gavin and I stayed up all night just talking about life and dreaming of our future. We talked about what we wanted our wedding to be like, the dessert we'd serve, and the honeymoon we would take. And then, despite all of my happiness, I simply started to cry.

"I can't believe I'm crying. I'm so happy and yet, I'm crying." I paused as I collected my thoughts. "I'll never forget that day Gavin. October second. I'll never forget it because it's the day everything changed. I changed. I feel like I'm a different person now. A sadder person, more reserved, more serious. And I'm crying now because it all seems too good to be true. How can I be so lucky to be engaged to the most amazing man in the world? You have always gone out of your way to make me feel so special. I just... I'm just scared. I loved Claire so much. She was my best friend and now I have you and I love you more than I've ever loved anyone. What if I lose you too? I just couldn't survive."

Gavin took my hand. "You can't go through life fearing that bad things are going to happen. That's not living. You worry now that I will die so you don't enjoy our time together. Then when we have kids and you will worry that something will happen to them. The fear will wear you down to the point that you don't see the good around you. What happened to Claire is horrible and I will forever hate that you've had to endure so much, but try to see the good. Think of Claire's journal. If you had never seen that journal, do you think you would've worked at camp? You wouldn't have met Nora and who knows what would've happened to her. You wouldn't have gone on a mission trip and met

Juan Jose and sponsored him and his siblings to go to school. You wouldn't have met Rosie and been a friend for her when she really needed one. And don't forget that that journal really brought us closer. Without that journal, we may not have started dating and we might not be here, engaged and sick from eating too much ice cream. Laura, you are not that scared fifteen year old anymore. You are a strong woman. You've grown and changed and I truly believe you were meant to find that journal but not for the same reason you think. All along, you've said that crossing items of the journal list allowed you to discover Claire but I think that more than anything, you discovered you. Losing Claire left you broken and lost. With this journal, you've found purpose in life. You are so devoted, so loving, and so kind. Yes, they were Claire's goals, but you accomplished them and even if Claire had accomplished them too, the experiences and the lessons you learned would have been different because you are different than Claire. You are Laura Russell."

That was the moment I realized that Gavin was right. Claire's journal was my path to rediscovering myself in a time when I felt purposeless and I'm eternally grateful for that gift and time I've had to learn more about Claire.

CHAPTER NINETEEN

Journal Entry:

    Someday I'll get married. I imagine to Kyle but I don't know. I love Kyle but maybe there's a different plan for me. When I do get married, I want to get married in spring when everything is fresh, beautiful, and new. I'd like to get married in my home church, the same church my parents got married in and where Laura and I were both baptized in. I'd like something simple yet beautiful. Short but sweet. Elegant but fun. I imagine a simple dress and ballet flats. My grandmother's pearl necklace from her own wedding. I envision cookies instead of cake and suits instead of tuxedos. We'd serve pizza and pasta over chicken and fish. Laura would be my maid of honor because not only is she my sister, she's always been my best friend. I remember once when we were kids. I think it was my twelfth or thirteenth birthday party; right around the time when girls started to be mean. Mom had said I could have my first boy-girl party so I invited three girlfriends and four boy friends, so that way the numbers would be equal. Everyone came, even James Kenzy, the boy I liked at the time. My mom had made us some cookies to have while we watched a movie in the basement. My dad had warned me not to have any "funny business." The movie started and my parents went upstairs. Within minutes, Jenna Anderson hit pause and said we should play truth or dare and that because I was the birthday girl, I had to go first. I chose dare and she dared me to kiss James in front of everyone. I was mortified. I had never kissed anyone before and didn't want to in front of everyone but I knew if I didn't they'd laugh and James would think I didn't like him. I decided to give James a peck on the cheek. Everyone laughed at me, even James. It was then that I realized friends come and go but that sisters are always there for you. And Laura has always been. That night of the party, I cried in my room and Laura came in and despite the age gap, she said the exact things I needed to hear. That's why I know, Laura will be my maid of honor and she'll always be my best friend.

Claire never got her day to walk with Daddy down the aisle. She never had her pizza, her cookies, or her ballet flats, but when my big day came, she was my maid of honor. After Gavin and I got engaged, mom had asked who my bridesmaids would be. I told her all I knew was that Claire was my honorary maid of honor. I think she thought I was crazy but it was exactly what I wanted.

Our wedding day was perfect, not because it was a beautiful fall day or the fact that I was able to fit into my grandmother's wedding dress. It was that after everything I've been through, I felt like I was finally starting fresh and anew and I was blessed enough to be able to begin this fresh start with a man I loved and who truly loved me. Although I wish Claire had been there and I cried because she couldn't, I know that she somehow had a hand in it because, throughout our adventures, Gavin too discovered Claire.

EPILOGUE

I stood silently gazing into the sunset near the Atlantic. Twenty years have gone by since I lost Claire, more of my life has been spent without her than with her. Despite that, she is always forefront in my mind. I may have forgotten what I wore that day and what I ate. I can't remember everything I did but I remember the essentials. I've lost those memories but how I felt will stay with me forever because at that moment on October 2, 2008, my life forever changed. I forever changed. The innocence of my childhood was ripped away and I was left with an overwhelming sense of how terrifying and unfair the world truly is.

It may have taken this long, but finally, I accomplished what I set out to do when I was fifteen years old. My journey took me from Wisconsin to amazing places in the world. I have had amazing adventures but I was never alone, my sister, Claire, has always been with me. A single tear streams down my face as I look up at Gavin. He squeezes my hand, and then I do the unthinkable, I whisper goodbye as I throw the book into the ocean. It may not be a true message in a bottle, but it was Claire's message to me. Her message saved my life because it gave me hope and purpose during a time I felt lost.

I hear the loud giggles behind us and turn to see our daughter Claire burying her twin brothers Johnny and Joey, who were adopted from Nicaragua, in the sand. If you had told me twenty years ago that life would still be worth living, I would have laughed at you but now as I look around at the people most important to me, I know that despite everything, I wouldn't change a thing because without the pain, I wouldn't be who I am today.

Oh wait, there was only one thing left to accomplish on the list: to write and publish a book. Being that you're reading this, I guess I succeeded at that too.